EX LIBRIS

VINTAGE **CLASSICS**

SIMONE DE BEAUVOIR

Simone de Beauvoir was born in Paris in 1908. In 1929 she became the youngest person ever to obtain the *agrégation* in philosophy at the Sorbonne, placing second to Jean-Paul Sartre. She taught at the lycées at Marseille and Rouen from 1931–1937, and in Paris from 1938–1943. After the war she emerged as one of the leaders of the existentialist movement, working with Sartre on *Les Temps Modernes*. The author of several books including *The Mandarins* (1954), which was awarded the Prix Goncourt, de Beauvoir was one of the most influential thinkers of her generation. She died in 1986.

ALSO BY SIMONE DE BEAUVOIR

FICTION

She Came to Stay
The Blood of Others
All Men are Mortal
The Mandarins
Les Belles Images
The Woman Destroyed
The Inseparables

NON-FICTION

The Ethics of Ambiguity
The Second Sex
Memoirs of a Dutiful Daughter
The Prime of Life
The Force of Circumstance
A Very Easy Death
All Said and Done
Adieux: A Farewell to Sartre
Letters to Sartre

SIMONE DE BEAUVOIR

Misunderstanding in Moscow

TRANSLATED FROM THE FRENCH BY
Terry Keefe

VINTAGE

1 3 5 7 9 10 8 6 4 2

Vintage Classics is part of the Penguin Random House group of companies
whose addresses can be found at global.penguinrandomhouse.com

Penguin
Random House
UK

This edition published in Vintage Classics in 2023
First published as *Malentendu à Moscou* by L'Herne in 2013

Copyright © Éditions de L'Herne 2013

Translation copyright © Terry Keefe 2011

penguin.co.uk/vintage-classics

Typeset in 12/16 pt Bembo Book MT Pro by Jouve (UK), Milton Keynes
Printed and bound in Great Britain by Clays Ltd, Elcograf S.p.A.

The authorised representative in the EEA is Penguin Random House Ireland,
Morrison Chambers, 32 Nassau Street, Dublin D02 YH68

A CIP catalogue record for this book is available from the British Library

ISBN 9781784878252

Penguin Random House is committed to a sustainable future
for our business, our readers and our planet. This book is made
from Forest Stewardship Council® certified paper.

MIX
Paper from
responsible sources
FSC
www.fsc.org   FSC® C018179

She looked up from her book. How irritating all these old refrains on noncommunication were! If we really want to communicate, we manage to do so more or less successfully. Not with everyone, of course, but with two or three people. André was sitting in the seat next to her, reading a thriller. She kept from him certain moods, some regrets, some little worries; doubtless he, too, had his own little secrets. But, by and large, there was nothing that they did not know about each other. She glanced through the plane window: dark forests and pale grassland stretching as far as one could see. How many times had they forged forward together, by train, by plane, by boat, sitting side by side, with books in their hands? There would still be many occasions when they would glide silently side by side over the sea, the earth and the air. This moment had the sweetness of a memory and the brightness of a promise. Were they thirty, or sixty? André's hair had turned white quite early, and at one time the snowy white colour that enhanced his fresh but matte complexion seemed stylish. It was still stylish. His skin had hardened and become lined, rather like old leather, but the smile at his mouth and in his eyes had kept its sparkle. His face today was preferable to that of his youth, despite what the photograph album might show. Nicole did not see him as having any particular age; probably because he himself seemed not to either. Although, in the past, he was so fond of running, swimming, climbing, and looking at himself in the mirror, he bore his sixty-four years nonchalantly. It was a long life behind them, with laughter, tears, moments of anger, caresses, confessions, silences, surges of affection [élans], and it sometimes seems that time has not passed by at all. The future still stretches out ahead, to infinity.

'Thank you.'

Nicole took a sweet from the basket, intimidated by the plumpness of the air hostess, and by the severity of her stare, just as she had been three years earlier by the restaurant waitresses and hotel chambermaids. You could only approve of their refusal to affect friendliness, and their keen awareness of their rights, but you felt yourself at fault in their presence, or at least suspect.

'We're landing,' she said.

She looked rather nervously at the ground coming up to meet them. An infinite future. But one that could be shattered from one minute to the next. She was very familiar with these sudden swings of mood, from smug security to pangs of fear: a Third World War was going to break out; André had contracted lung cancer – two packets of cigarettes a day was too many, far too many; or the plane was about to smash into the ground. That would've been a good way for it all to end: no complications, and with the two of them together. But not so soon, not now.

'We made it safely again,' she said to herself once the wheels hit the runway, albeit rather violently. The travellers put on their coats, gathered their hand luggage. They were standing around waiting, standing around for some time.

'Can you smell the birch trees?' André asked.

It was very cool, almost cold: 61°F according to the air hostess's announcement. How close Paris was, at three and a half hours of flight time, and yet how far away. This morning Paris had been sweltering under the first great heat wave of the summer, with the smell of asphalt and a storm in the air. How close Philippe was, and yet how far away . . .

A bus took them — across an aerodrome that was much more extensive than the one at which they had landed in 1963 — to a glazed building in the shape of a mushroom, where the passports were checked. Macha was waiting for them at the exit. Once again Nicole was surprised to see, harmoniously blended in her face, the very dissimilar features of Claire and André. She was slim and elegant: only her over-permed hairstyle marked her as a Muscovite.

'How was the flight? Are you [*vous*] well? And how are you [*tu*]?'

She addressed her father informally, Nicole formally. It was to be expected, and yet at the same time peculiar.

'Hand me your bag.'

That was to be expected, too. But when a man carries your bags, it's because you are a woman: when a woman does, it's because she is younger than you, and you feel old.

'Give me the luggage slips and sit there,' Macha said authoritatively. Nicole obeyed. She was old. With André she often forgot the fact, but dozens of little irritations periodically reminded her of it.

'An attractive young woman!' she had thought, on spotting Macha. She remembered having smiled at the age of thirty when her father-in-law had used those very words to describe a forty-year-old. She, too, now found that most people seemed young. She was old. And she wasn't accepting the fact very easily (the combination of astonishment and distress that she felt was one of the rare things that she kept from André). She told herself: 'In any case, there are some advantages.' Being retired sounded a little like being on the scrap heap, but it was pleasant to take your vacation whenever you wanted; or, more precisely, to be on vacation all the time. Sweltering in their classrooms, her ex-colleagues would be beginning to dream of getting away. And she herself had already left. She looked around for André, who was standing in the crowd, next to Macha. In Paris, he allowed himself to be put upon by too many people. As much as he possibly could, he was always ready to come to the aid of Spanish political prisoners; Portuguese detainees; persecuted Israelis; rebels in the Congo, in Angola, in Cameroon; Venezuelan, Peruvian, Colombian partisans. And there were others she was forgetting. Meetings, manifestos, rallies, tracts, delegations – he took on all kinds of tasks. He belonged to a great many groups and committees. But here no one would be asking anything of him. Macha was the only person they knew. They would have nothing to do but look at things together: she loved discovering things with him and finding that time, usually static in the well-established routine of their happiness, could again become an outpouring of new experiences. She stood up. She would have liked to be out in the streets already, under the walls of the Kremlin. She had forgotten how long the waiting could be in this country.

'Is our luggage coming?'

'It'll come eventually,' said André.

Three and a half hours, he thought. How close Moscow was, yet at the same time so far! Why, at just three and a half hours away, did he see Macha so rarely? (But there were so many obstacles, not least the cost of the journey.)

'It's a long time, three years,' he said. 'I must look older.'

'Not at all. You haven't changed.'

'You look even more beautiful than ever.'

He looked at her with great delight. You think that nothing can happen to you any more; you have even resigned yourself to the fact (and that hadn't been easy, although he hadn't let it show). And then along comes a wholly new major affection, which lights up your life. He had scarcely taken any interest in the frightened little girl – she was called Maria at the time – whom Claire used to bring to see him for a few hours from Japan, Brazil, or Moscow. And the young woman who had come to Paris after the war to introduce her husband had remained a stranger to him. But during Macha's second trip, in 1960, something had happened between them. He didn't quite understand why she had become attached to him in such an extreme way, but it had moved him. Nicole's love for him remained alive, attentive, joyous, but they were too used to each other for André to be able to awaken in her the sparkling happiness that, at this very moment, was transforming the rather severe features of Macha.

'Is our luggage coming?' asked Nicole.

'It'll come eventually,' said André.

What was the point of being impatient? They had plenty of time at their disposal here. In Paris, André was tortured by how fast the hours flew by, torn between appointments; especially since his retirement, for he had overestimated how much leisure time he would have. Out of curiosity, and because he had not thought things through, he had allowed himself to take on a raft of obligations from which he could not manage to free himself. He was going to escape from them for a month; he would be able to live in the carefree way that he liked so much; that he liked too much, since it was exactly what caused most of his worries.

'Here are our bags,' he said.

They put them into Macha's car and she got into the

driver's seat. She drove slowly, like everyone here. There was the smell of fresh greenery during their drive; whole fleets of tree-trunks were drifting down the Moscova; and André felt welling up inside him the emotion without which life for him would have been completely lacking in spice. He was at the beginning of an adventure which excited and frightened him, an adventure of discovery. He had never been concerned with succeeding, or being someone. (If his mother had not imperiously devoted herself to ensuring that he pursued his studies, he would have been perfectly content with the same status as his parents, that of primary-school teachers in the sunshine of Provence.) It seemed to him that the truth of his existence and what he was did not rest with him: it was mysteriously scattered across the whole world. To know it, he had to find out about the past and different places: that was why he loved history and travelling. But while he could serenely study the past as refracted in books, approaching an unknown country – which, in its living profusion, would go beyond everything that he could know about it – always made him giddy. And this one was of more concern to him than any other. He had been brought up in the cult of Lenin: his mother, at 83, was still a militant in the ranks of the Communist Party. He himself had not become a member, but he had always thought, through the turmoils of both hope and despair, that the USSR held the key to the future, and hence to the present era and his own destiny. Yet never, even in the dark years of Stalinism, had he had the impression of being so far from understanding the country. Was this stay going to cast any light on it? In 1963, they had travelled as tourists – to the Crimea and Sotchi – looking at things superficially. This time he would ask questions, he would have the newspapers read to him, he would mix with crowds. The car turned into Gorky Street. There were people, shops. Would he manage to feel at home here? The thought of failing threw him into a panic.

'I should have studied Russian more seriously!' he said to himself.

Another of the things that he had promised himself he would do, but hadn't done: he hadn't got beyond the sixth lesson of the Assimil course.

Nicole was right to call him a lazy old thing. He always felt up to reading, talking, going walking, but he had no stomach for unrewarding tasks like learning vocabulary, or taking systematic notes. In that case, he shouldn't be taking the world so much to heart. He was too serious and too frivolous.

'That's the contradiction in me,' he cheerfully told

himself. (He had been delighted to hear the expression from the lips of an Italian colleague, who was a convinced Marxist and yet oppressed his wife.) In truth, he didn't feel at all bad about himself.

The railway station, painted in a garish green: Muscovite green. ('If you don't like that, you don't like Moscow,' André had said, three years earlier.)

Gorky Street. The Peking Hotel: a modest, tiered wedding cake when you compared it with the gigantic, ornate buildings allegedly inspired by the Kremlin, with which the city was bristling. Nicole remembered everything. And as soon as she got out of the car she recognised the smell of Moscow, an even stronger smell of diesel fumes than in 1963, doubtless because there were far more vehicles, especially trucks and vans.

'Was it three years ago already?' she asked herself as she went into the large, bare entrance lobby. (There was a greyish sheet over the newspaper-seller's stall; people were lining up at the door of the restaurant, with its extravagant Chinese décor.)

How quickly the three years had gone by. It was frightening. How many more three years were there left in her life? Nothing had changed, except that for foreigners – Macha had forewarned them – the formerly derisory charges for rooms had tripled. The woman attendant on the fourth floor gave them a key. All along the long corridor Nicole sensed her stare on the back of her neck. They were lucky to have curtains at the windows of their room: often it was just bare window-panes in the hotels. (Macha didn't have proper curtains at home, just light net curtains. She said that you get used to it, and that she would even have found it difficult to sleep in complete darkness.)

Down below, work on the broad avenue was complete and the cars were surging down into a tunnel under Mayakovsky Square. The crowds on the pavements were wearing summer colours: it was June and they imagined it was hot!

'Here are some things for you,' Nicole said to Macha as she began to unpack her suitcase.

Some recent novels, some Pléiade volumes, some records. And also some cardigans, stockings, blouses: Macha loved clothes. She found it a joy to touch and feel the wool and the silk; she compared one shade of colour with another. Nicole went into the bathroom. Another stroke of luck: the two taps and the flushing toilet all worked. She changed her dress and touched up her make-up.

'What a pretty dress!' Macha said.

'I'm very fond of it.'

At the age of 50, her outfits always seemed either too sad or too gay for her. But now she knew what she ought and ought not to wear; what she wore was no problem to her. But it gave her no pleasure either. The intimate, almost tender relationship that she formerly had with her clothes no longer existed. She hung up her suit in the wardrobe; although she had been wearing it for two years, it was an ordinary, impersonal object that carried nothing of herself within it. Meanwhile, Macha was smiling into the mirror, not at the pretty blouse that she had just put on, but at an unexpected and attractive incarnation of herself.

'Yes, I can remember that,' Nicole said to herself.

'I've reserved a table at the Praga,' Macha said. She had remembered that it was Nicole's favourite restaurant: she's so considerate, and has a memory as well organised as mine. Nicole could understand the affection that André had for her. All the more so as he had always wanted a daughter; he bore something of a grudge against Philippe for being a boy.

It took Macha only ten minutes to drive them to the Praga. They left their coats in the cloakroom, which was a compulsory ritual: you were forbidden to go into a restaurant with a coat on your back or over your arm. They sat down in a dining room with a flagstone floor, full of palm trees and greenery, with a large purplish landscape painting covering the whole of one wall.

'How much vodka?' Macha asked. 'I'm driving, so I won't drink.'

'Order three hundred grams in any case,' André said.

He looked towards Nicole. 'Since it's our first evening?'

'All right. Since it's our first evening,' she said, with a smile.

He tended to drink in the way that he smoked, to excess. As far as tobacco was concerned, she had given up the struggle, but she managed to moderate his drinking habits.

'Since it's our first evening, I'll forget my diet,' she said. 'I'll have caviar and chicken julienne.'

'Are you on a diet?'

'Yes, for the last six months. I was putting on weight.'

Perhaps she ate more than before she retired; in any case, she was getting less exercise. Philippe had said to her one day, 'Well, fancy that: you're filling out.' (Since then, he had scarcely seemed to notice that she had become thinner.) And, to make matters worse, all that people could talk about in Paris this year was keeping one's figure, or getting it back: low calories, carbohydrates, miracle drugs.

'You look fine,' said Macha.

'I've lost five kilos. And I'm making sure that I don't put them back on. I weigh myself every day.'

Some years ago, she had never imagined that she would ever worry about her weight. But now that's what it had come to! The less easily she was able to identify with her body, the more she felt obliged to pay attention to it. She was responsible for it and she looked after it with a kind of worried devotion, in the way she might have looked after an old friend who had become slightly unattractive, diminished, and who needed her.

'Well, Philippe is getting married then?' Macha said. 'What's his fiancée like?'

'Pretty, and intelligent,' André said.

'I don't like her at all,' said Nicole.

Macha started to laugh.

'You certainly said that with feeling! I've never known a mother-in-law who liked her daughter-in-law.'

'She's the "super woman" type,' said Nicole.

'There are a lot like that in Paris. They have some sort of career, they claim to dress well, to engage in sports, look after their house perfectly, bring up their children very well. They want to prove to themselves that they can be successful at all levels. And, in fact, they spread themselves too thinly, they succeed in nothing. Young women of that kind make my blood run cold.'

'You're being a little unfair,' said André.

'Maybe.'

She talked about places with Nicole: Novgorod, Pskoff, Rostov the Great, Leningrad. Nicole wanted to be on the move and that was fine: it was largely to please him that she had come to the USSR and he wanted it to be a pleasant trip for her. He looked at them, and felt a glow of warmth. Macha had much more in common with Nicole than with Claire, who was pretty but empty-headed, and, fortunately, had been as anxious as he was to get divorced once their child had been made legitimate. He was pleased that they got along so well together, the two people he loved most in the world. (As far as Philippe was concerned, he had never been able to rid himself of a certain jealousy. Too often he found himself as the third person, coming between Nicole and her son.) Nicole counted much more to him than Macha, but when he was with Macha he had this feeling that he would never again have experienced without her: a kind of romantic feeling. Nothing was stopping him from having new affairs. One fine day Nicole had announced that she considered herself too old for sexual pleasures. (It was absurd: he loved her just as fully today as he used to.)

Accordingly, she had granted him his freedom. In fact, she would still have been quite capable of fits of jealousy; and they no longer had enough time left to live to waste it in quarrelling. Then again, in spite of gymnastic exercises and severe self-restraint, he no longer liked his body: it was no gift to give to a woman. His chastity didn't torment him (except upon reflection, when he recognised his indifference as a mark of his age). But neither was there any pleasure in the thought: 'It's all over. Life holds nothing unexpected for me any more.' Then Macha had come along, and was still there.

'Isn't your husband going to be angry that we're taking you away from him?' he asked.

'Youri's never angry,' Macha said cheerfully.

According to their conversation in the Praga, it seemed that her feelings for Youri were more a matter of friendship than of love. But, all in all, it was lucky that he more or less suited her: she had married him on impulse, in order to be able to stay in the USSR, since she was sickened by the circles that her mother and step-father mixed in, and by the capitalist world in general. This had become her country: that was part of what gave her such prestige in André's eyes.

'What's the situation like culturally this year?'

'The same as ever. We're struggling on.'

She was in what she called the liberal camp, which was fighting against academicism, dogmatism, the vestiges of Stalinism.

Once again she asked herself: Why Irène? I thought that when he got married . . . I thought that he wouldn't get married, that he would remain the little boy who had said to me, like all little boys: 'When I'm grown up, I'll marry you.' Then one evening he had said, 'I've got some great news for you!' in the overexcited manner of a child who, on some public holiday, has been playing for too long, laughing too much, shouting too much. And Nicole had experienced that heaviness in her chest, that flushing of her cheeks, the straining of all her muscles to prevent her lips from trembling.

One February evening, with the curtains drawn, and the lights picking out the rainbow colours of the cushions, suddenly his impending absence had opened up an abyss: 'He will be living with another woman, somewhere else.' Well, yes, it's true! I'll have to resign myself to it, she told herself. The vodka was iced, the caviar a velvety grey in colour, she liked Macha, and she was going to have André all to herself for a month. She felt very happy.

He felt very happy sitting in an armchair between the two beds, with Macha propped up on one side and Nicole on the other. (In 1963, Youri was away on an archaeological trip; he had taken Vassili with him and Macha's apartment was empty. This year, for them to spend the evening alone with her, they had no alternative but to use their hotel bedroom.)

'I've arranged things so that I can be free for the whole month,' Macha said.

She worked for a publisher who published Russian classics in French, in Moscow, and contemporary texts in a journal that went out to various foreign countries. She translated, but she also acted as a reader, choosing and recommending.

'We could leave for Vladimir at the end of the week,' she continued. 'It's three hours away by car.'

'And are you winning?'

'Sometimes. There's a rumour that certain scholars are getting ready to shatter the sacrosanct idea of a dialectic of nature. That would be a great victory.'

'It's good to have something to fight for,' he said.

'You fight for things, too,' Nicole said sharply.

'No. Not since the Algerian War. I try to be of some help; it's not the same thing. What's more, it's almost always futile.'

Since 1962, he had lost all hold on the world. That was

perhaps why he was so restless, because he was not acting any more. His powerlessness – that of the French Left as a whole – sometimes depressed him. Especially first thing in the morning, when, instead of getting up, he would bury himself in the bedclothes, pulling the sheet over his head until the moment when he remembered an urgent meeting and leapt out of bed.

'Then why do you do it?' said Macha.

'I can see no reason for not doing it.'

'You could do your own work. Those articles that you were talking about three years ago . . .'

'I didn't write them. Nicole will tell you that I'm a lazy old thing.'

'Not at all!' said Nicole. 'You live in the way that you want to. Why force yourself?'

Is that what she thought? She didn't press him in the way that she used to, but that was probably because she had given up the struggle. She wouldn't have attached so much importance to her son's thesis if she hadn't been a little disappointed with her husband. Too bad.

'In any case, it's a pity,' said Macha.

In his head, he kept hearing the same thing: it's a pity. He had resigned himself to Nicole's regrets, but he would have liked to present to Macha an image of himself other than that of an old retiree who has done nothing. He had had some ideas on the subject of certain contemporary events that Nicole found interesting. Several times he had promised himself that he would look into them more deeply. But it was the present that consumed him: he didn't want to turn back towards the past before he had finished understanding the world of today. And what time it took to keep up to date with things!

Still, he had thought that the day would come when this investigation would be complete, and then he would be able to follow through the projects that he had enthusiastically outlined and – provisionally – abandoned. That day had not come, and would not come. He realised that now: the task was an infinite one. Year by year he became better informed, yet found himself to be more ignorant. The obscurities, difficulties and contradictions were multiplying around him. China seemed much more impenetrable to him than in 1950. The foreign policy of the USSR disconcerted him.

'It's not too late,' Macha went on, in an encouraging tone, as if she were afraid of having upset him.

'No, it's not too late,' he said brightly.

It was too late; he would not change. In fact, if, like Philippe, he had been able to discipline himself, he would have been able at one and the same time to gather information about the present and go more deeply into a particular historical question. But any constraint made him bristle, perhaps because he had been subject to too many during his childhood. He had retained a taste for playing truant, and seeking adventures – something that was so severely punished and all the more delicious as a result. He had never sincerely reproached himself for his laziness: it arose out of his openness to the world, out of his determination to remain available. Suddenly, seen through the eyes of Macha, it looked like something quite different: an oddity, a habit, a flaw that marked him indelibly. He had given in to it; it sprang from within himself. And now, even if he wanted to, he could not overcome it.

'It's touching, the way Macha is fond of you,' said Nicole, when they were alone together again.

'I wonder why,' he said. 'I think Youri is more of a comrade than a support to her. She wanted a father. When she came to Paris in 1960 she had decided to love me.'

'Don't be so modest,' said Nicole, laughing.

'I loved you without having decided to do so.'

'I was young.'

'You haven't aged.'

He did not protest. Nicole seemed not to be conscious

of her age. He did not talk about his own age, but he thought about it often, being horrified by it. For a long time – in bad faith, thoughtlessly, by pulling the wool over his own eyes – he had refused to consider himself an adult. The teacher, the father, the fifty-year-old, he wasn't really any of these things. Now here he was with his life closing in around him; neither the past nor the future could offer him excuses any more. He was a sixty-year-old, an old retiree who had done nothing. Well, he might as well be that as anything else. The regrets that he had begun to entertain had already vanished. Had he been a lecturer at the Sorbonne and a well-known historian, he would have found himself with the weight of that other destiny behind him and it would not have been any lighter to bear. What was horrifying was to find himself defined, static, formed; to find that the ephemeral moments accumulate and form a matrix around you in which you are trapped. He kissed Nicole and climbed into bed. At least there was still dreaming. He put his cheek on the pillow.

He liked to feel himself slipping away into sleep. His dreams involved more radical changes of scenery than any book or film. Their very gratuitousness delighted him. Except in those dreadful nightmares when all his teeth crumbled in his mouth, he did not have a particular age in his dreams; he escaped from time. His dreams doubtless were situated in his own history; they flourished on his past. But in a way that was mysterious to him, and they did not go on into the future. They constituted a pure present and he could forget them. From one night to the next they vanished; they sprang up without accumulating: a source of eternal novelty.

'I would still like to understand why they ban foreigners from going to Vladimir by car,' said André.

The train was travelling fast, and smoothly; but all the seats in the coach were facing backward and Nicole was unable to travel backward without her stomach protesting. (How humiliating that had been at the stage when she was trying to rival boys in matters of health, strength and endurance!) She had her knees under her on the seat and was trying to face André and Macha: this eventually became gruelling.

'What you must understand is that there is nothing to understand,' said Macha. 'It's a good road, and the villages that you go through are thriving. It's just bureaucratic absurdity, against the old background of mistrust of foreigners.'

'Kindness and mistrust: it's a strange mixture,' said Nicole.

That was what had disconcerted them in 1963. Standing in line – in front of the Mausoleum, at the Goum, or at the door of a restaurant – Macha had only to say a word for people to step aside to let them through. Yet in the Crimea they had come across prohibitions everywhere: the east coast and Sebastopol were prohibited areas for foreigners. Intourist had claimed that the mountain road linking Yalta and Simferopol was being repaired, but Macha had been told in confidence that it was, in fact, closed only to foreigners.

'You're not too tired?' André asked.

'I can manage.'

She was rather worn out, but she forgot her tiredness as she watched the countryside race by, vast and quiet, softened by the light from a sunset that was never-ending. She had just had four splendid days. Moscow had changed a little, was somewhat uglier. (What a pity that changes are almost always for the worse, for places as well as for people.) They had discovered some avenues for the first time, gone all over ancient quarters of the city.

Red Square, closed to motor vehicles, seemed bigger and more solemn: a holy place. Unfortunately, whereas Saint Basil's Church used to rise up into the sky, a huge hotel behind it now blocked off the horizon. Nevertheless, Nicole had been delighted to see the churches of the Kremlin again, as well as the icons there and in the museums. There were still a great many old houses that she found charming, especially in the evening, when you could glimpse through the windows and a screen of green plants the warm light from an old-fashioned lampshade, made of orange or pink silk, with fringes.

'Here we are at Vladimir,' said Macha.

They left their luggage at the hotel. It was too late to dine there: Macha had decided that they would picnic outside. The sky was still pink and a full round moon had risen. They followed a path that ran alongside the Kremlin ramparts: beneath them was a river, the train station, flickering lights. There was a church in the garden that they crossed, with its scent of phlox and petunias; lovers were embracing on benches.

'We could stop here,' Nicole said.

'A little further on is better,' said Macha.

She gave orders, they obeyed. It amused Nicole, because she was not used to taking orders. They kept walking and went into another garden surrounding another church.

'Let's sit here,' said Macha. 'This is the most beautiful church in Vladimir.'

The church was slim and slender in a white dress covered

with embroidery half way up, and crowned by a single, golden onion-shaped dome. Its simplicity shone out brightly. They sat down and Macha unpacked their food.

'I'll have just two hard-boiled eggs,' said Nicole.

'Aren't you hungry?'

'Yes, but I don't want to put on weight.'

'Oh, don't be obsessive!' said Macha. 'You must eat a little more than that!'

Macha's indignant, gruff voice made Nicole smile: no one spoke to her in that tone. She bit into a *pirozhok*.

'Are Youri and Vassili as docile as I am?'

'They're quite docile,' said Macha cheerfully.

'Try to intimidate your father then. Tell him that he risks lung cancer by smoking forty cigarettes a day.'

'Get lost, both of you,' said André in a polite tone.

'It's true that you smoke too much,' Macha said.

'Pass me the vodka then.'

Macha filled the paper cups and for a while they ate and drank in silence.

'The church is beautiful,' said André with a tinge of regret in his voice.

'I'm looking at it as hard as I can, and I know that in a week's time I won't remember it any more.'

'Neither will I,' said Nicole.

Yes, she would forget the golden and white church; she had forgotten so much! Her curiosity, which was still virtually intact, often seemed to her no more than a crazy relic: what was the point of it when memories crumble into dust? The moon was shining, as was the little star which faithfully accompanies it, and Nicole repeated to herself the lovely lines from Aucassin and Nicolette: 'I see you tiny star. Drawn closely to the moon.' That's the advantage of literature, she told herself: you can take words around with you. Images fade, become distorted, disappear. But she could still find the old words in her throat, precisely as they had been written. They linked her to former centuries, when the stars shone in exactly the way they do today.

And this rebirth, this permanence gave her an impression of eternity. The earth was worn down, yet there were moments like this, when it seemed as fresh as in primordial times, and when the present was self-sufficient. Nicole was here, she was looking at the church: for no reason, simply in order to see it. Warmed by a few mouthfuls of vodka, she found this very disinterestedness poignant and charming.

They went back to the hotel. There were no curtains, but Nicole tied a scarf around her head and quickly fell asleep. Tender waking moments.

In the bedroom, now flooded with light, André was

curled up on the bed, blindfolded like a condemned man, with his hand pressed against the wall in an infantile way, as if, during a disturbed sleep, he had needed to experience the solidity of the world. How many times had she sat – how many times would she sit in the future – on the edge of the bed, putting her hand on his shoulder, shaking him gently? Sometimes he murmured, 'Good morning, mommy,' and then he shook himself and smiled in a dazed manner. She put her hand on his shoulder.

'I want to show you something,' said Macha, pushing open the door of a church. She led them through the semi-darkness. 'Look at the fate reserved for foreigners.'

The fresco represented the Last Judgment. On the right, angels and some of the chosen few in ageless long robes; on the left, condemned to hell, French people in period costumes, with black doublets, breeches tied above the calf, lace ruffles, little pointed beards, and behind them, Muslims in turbans.

'It really is an old tradition,' said Nicole.

'Actually,' said Macha, 'except for a few rare periods, Russia has been broadly open to the West. But in certain quarters there has always been hostility, particularly in the Church. Notice that they are damned as infidels, not because of their nationality.'

'In practice, it amounts to the same thing,' said André.

He was in a bad mood this morning. The previous day had been delightful. He liked Vladimir, with its churches and the Roublov frescoes. And eating badly did not matter to him: his mother had brought him up well. But the discussion that he had started with Macha irritated him. Until then, he had been firmly convinced that she shared his views.

'Your nationalism won't be easily dislodged,' he continued, as they came out of the church. 'The gist of what you have just explained is that you are no longer a revolutionary country and that that's fine.'

'Not at all. We have had the revolution and it is not in question. But in France you don't know what war is. We do. We don't want it.'

Macha had spoken angrily and André, too, felt annoyed.

'No one wants it. What I'm saying is that if you give America a free hand, if you don't stop the escalation, that's when America is to be feared. Munich prevented nothing at all.'

'Do you think that if we bomb the American bases, the USA won't retaliate? We won't take that risk.'

'If they attack China, will you still not make a move?'

'Oh, you're not going to start again!' said Nicole.

'You've been arguing for two hours: neither of you is going to persuade the other.'

They walked on for a moment in silence. The streets were full of people. It was the Birch-Tree Festival; doubtless a substitute for Corpus Christi. People had danced until midnight in a huge open-air enclosure (there were neither tables, nor chairs, just a dance-floor surrounded by a fence). Early in the morning there had been a procession on the central avenue: trucks with girls in white dresses and boys in red ties, holding birch branches in their hands. They were singing. In the park, a pavilion had been turned into a buffet: there were little tables outside, large ones inside, and on them piles of cakes and rolls.

'Let's sit down and eat something,' Macha suggested.

'Oh, yes! If we can eat, let's eat,' said Nicole.

On the previous day, in Vladimir, there was a food shortage. The restaurant was not serving fish, or mutton, or poultry, or vegetables, or fruit: just stews that Nicole and Macha found inedible. The bread, which was neither white nor black, tasted like glue. In front of the hotel, people were lining up to buy pancakes hard enough to break your teeth. And there they were this morning, with women coming out of the pavilion loaded with garlands of pretzels and their shopping bags stuffed full of food. They ordered cakes and egg and cheese sandwiches, which were excellent.

'Nothing to eat in the towns, and here as much as one wants. How has that come about?' asked André.

'I've told you that you mustn't try to understand,' said Macha.

According to her, they were not to be surprised by any incoherence, any absurdity. The country was still hampered by a fossilised bureaucratic machine, which was responsible for enormous wastage and paralysing decisions.

The government was doing its best by all possible means to combat this inertia, but it would take time to win the battle.

'Remember the story of the school chairs,' she continued.

The previous morning, she had come out of the hotel doubled up with laughter, because of the programme that she had just heard on Vladimir radio station. One factory made chair backs, another the seats, and a third assembled them. But, for one thing, there was always a shortage of either seats or backs; and, for another, whenever an attempt was made to fit the two pieces together, one of them broke. After a series of steps and measures, enquiries, checks, reports, it had been concluded that the assembly procedure was faulty. But they had to go around a vast administrative circuit before authorisation to modify it could be given. 'It's pure absurdity,' Macha had said, pointing out at the same time that in putting out this story the radio was contributing to the struggle against bureaucracy. She was very free in her judgments of the régime, being critical and discriminating. If she approved of its foreign policy, therefore, it was not out of blind compliance, and this disturbed André all the more. But he did not want to talk about it again, for the moment. He looked at the crowd all around him: people's faces were shining with gaiety, as if they had participated willingly in the processions, the ceremonies, the whole of this festival. And yet they seemed firmly supervised; they were obeying instructions. Gaiety and discipline: there is no contradiction. But he would have liked to know how the two things were reconciled. Probably in different ways according to people's ages and circumstances. If only he had been able to understand what they were saying!

'You ought to give us Russian lessons,' he said to Macha.

'Oh, no!' said Nicole. 'I don't even know the alphabet. How much do you expect me to learn in a month? But you take lessons if you'd like to,' she added.

'You'll be bored while I'm doing so.'

'Of course not. I'll read.'

'Fine! Tomorrow, in Moscow, we'll make a start,' André said. 'Perhaps I shall feel a little less lost.'

'Because you feel lost?'

'Completely.'

'Those will be your first words when you get to heaven – or hell: "I feel completely lost,"' Nicole said, smiling at him affectionately. She had always smiled at his confusion. When they were travelling, she accepted things as they were presented to her. 'Well, what do you expect! It's Africa and this is a colony!' she said to him at Gardhaia. (André was still quite young, and it was his first encounter with the Maghreb. There were camels and veiled women, but also canned food and hardware in the shops. It was both distant Arabia and a French village: he could not manage to grasp what it was like for the men he came across to belong to both.) The reasons for his present confusion were much more serious. What did it feel like to be someone from the Soviet Union? To what extent did the singing young people on these avenues resemble French young people; in what respects were they different? In their minds, how did the will to construct, socialism, and national self-interest blend together? Much depended on the answers that could be given to these questions.

'You're wrong to talk of self-interest,' Macha said to him a few hours later.

In the room where they were drinking tea, resting after a long walk, she had taken up the morning's conversation again, but in a more relaxed tone.

'Atomic war doesn't involve just us, but the whole world. You must understand that we are torn between two imperatives: helping socialism across the world and preserving the peace. We don't want to abandon either.'

'Oh! I'm well aware that the situation isn't a simple one.'

'Then why don't you leave it at that?' Nicole said quickly. 'Macha wants me to look at her translation with her. It we don't do it immediately, we won't have time.'

'Yes, we must get down to it,' said Macha.

They sat side by side at the table. He opened a guide to the USSR that he had brought from Paris and pretended to be absorbed in it, but his thoughts continued to go around in circles. It was true that one could not rule out the possibility of a terrifying American retaliation for any attempt to counter their escalation. What followed from this?

In 1945, the atomic bomb was only a fairly abstract threat: now it had become an anguishing possibility. There were people who were not worried by it: 'If I have to die, whether the world survives or not is all the same to me.' One of André's friends had even said, 'If it comes to it, I shall have fewer regrets if I can think that I'm leaving nothing behind.' He himself would have killed himself at once if he had known that the world was going to be blown up. Or just that the whole of civilisation would be destroyed, that historical continuity would be broken and that the survivors – doubtless Chinese people – would start up again from scratch. Perhaps they would enable socialism to triumph, but their version of it would bear no relation to the one that his parents, his comrades and he himself had dreamed of. Yet if the USSR settled down to peaceful co-existence, socialism would be a long time coming. How many hopes had been disappointed! The Popular Front, the Resistance in France; and the emancipation of the Third World, which had not pushed back capitalism by a single inch. The Chinese Revolution had resulted in the Sino-Soviet conflict. No, the future had never seemed so bleak to André. 'My life will have served no purpose,' he thought. What he had wanted was for it to be usefully incorporated into a history that led men towards happiness. Doubtless they would find happiness one day; André had believed in that for too long not to still believe in it a little. But it would come about in such a roundabout way that history would have stopped being his history.

Nicole's voice broke into his reflections.

'Macha's French is entirely correct; even a little too correct, a little stilted.'

'I'm so afraid of making mistakes,' said Macha.

'One can sense that.'

Once more they bent over the typed sheets, smiling at each other and whispering. Nicole, who was usually so hard on women, felt a real friendship for Macha; André was delighted by how well they got along.

'I'd like to look at the translation, too,' he said. Even if the future seemed bleak, he must not spoil this moment of tender intimacy. He tore himself away from his ruminations.

'I'd be glad to sit down,' said Nicole.

The Uzbek restaurant was charming, with its little open-air enclosures and its exotic clientele: men with flat faces and slanting eyes, wearing square hats; women with heavy black braids, in multicoloured silk dresses. You could eat the best *chachliks* in Moscow there. But the din of the orchestra – and it was the same everywhere – had driven them away as soon as they had swallowed their last mouthful. Macha had suggested a walk. And, since they had walked a great deal during the day, Nicole felt tired. It was annoying: she used to be able to go on for miles, as merrily as André! Now, every evening after their long rambles her legs gave out on her. She did not let it show. But, after all, it was stupid to force oneself.

They were going past an empty bench – a rare windfall – and she might as well profit from it.

They sat down.

'Well, then, in the end are we able to go to Rostov the Great, or not?'

'I'm afraid not,' said Macha.

'And our little trip on the Moskva?'

'I can ask . . .'

'Oh, why don't we simply stay in Moscow!' said André. 'There are so many things that we want to see again.'

'We shall see them again in any case.'

Seeing things again – there had been a time, when she was nearly forty, when that delighted her. But not before that, when she badly needed novelty.

Just as she did now. So few years left to live: walking about in Red Square day after day was a waste of time. It was a wonderful square: what an unexpected impact it had made, three years ago. This year, too, on the first day. But already Nicole knew it too well. That was the great difference between their first trip and this one. In 1963, everything was new; this time, almost nothing was. That was probably the source of her slight disappointment.

'And where are we going to spend the evening?' she asked.

'Why not here?' said André.

'On this bench, all evening?'

This year, they did not know where to go in the evenings. Youri seemed very nice – since he did not speak French, relations with him were rather basic – but he worked in his room, and Vassili in his. They had to whisper in order not to disturb the two of them, and, even so, felt that they were intruding. The hotel room was not welcoming. Many cafés had been built in the intervening three years. With their glass walls, they were not ugly from the outside, but inside they were like cheese shops, lacking comfort and intimacy. In any case, by this time of day they were closed. Would it be this bench, then, next to a subway station, in a square smelling of diesel fumes?

'We're fine here,' said André. 'There's a smell of greenery in the air.'

He was fine anywhere. He was not cold in his flannel suit, and Macha found it warm at any temperature over 50°F but Nicole was shivering in her light silk dress. Also, to spend the whole evening on a bench was to feel like the victim of a disaster.

'I'm cold,' she said.

'We can go to the bar in the National,' said Macha.

'Good idea.'

The bar stayed open until two o'clock in the morning; you could pay in foreign currency and have whisky, as well as American cigarettes. She had pointed this out to André and Macha on the day when they lunched there, but they had not responded. Still, Macha had made a mental note of it and she remembered it at the appropriate time. They got up.

'Is it far?'

'Half an hour's walk. Perhaps we'll find a taxi,' said Macha.

Nicole wanted a taxi: her legs and feet were hurting. Usually, you could easily find one: there were twice as many as in 1963. This evening quite a number were going by, with their little green eye illuminated in a promising way, but however much you signalled to them they kept moving on relentlessly: they were not allowed to stop on these big avenues. The nearest taxi rank was some distance away; and perhaps there would be a line and no vehicles. Walking and sitting on benches was quite a tough regimen.

Moscow was perhaps fine for its inhabitants; Macha would not have wanted to live anywhere else, especially not in Paris (which was surprising, all the same). But how austere it all was for foreigners! Perhaps I've grown old in the last three years, Nicole thought to herself; I am less good at putting up with discomfort. And that will only get worse. 'We're in the flower of old age,' said André. A strange kind of flower – more like prickly thistles.

'I'm dead tired,' she said.

'We're almost there.'

'It's no fun, getting old.'

Macha had taken her arm. 'Come on! You're so young, both of you.'

People often said that to her: 'You seem so young'; 'You're young.' An ambiguous compliment, which heralds painful times to come. To stay young is to retain some vitality, some cheerfulness, some presence of mind. What awaits the old, therefore, is routine, gloom, senility. They say: 'Old age doesn't exist; it's nothing.' Or even: 'It's very beautiful, very moving.' But when they encounter it, they discreetly cover it up, with words that lie. Macha said: 'You're young.' But she had taken Nicole's arm. Basically, it was because of Macha that Nicole had been feeling her age so acutely since she arrived. She realised that she had hung onto the image of herself that she had at the age of forty. She recognised herself in the vigorous young woman that was Macha, all the more so as Macha exuded experience and authority, and was as mature as Nicole; they were peers. And then, all of a sudden, a gesture, an inflection of Macha's voice, a considerate action reminded her that there was an age difference of twenty years between them – and that she was sixty.

'What a crowd!' said André.

The bar was smoky and rowdy. There was one free table, wedged between some young Americans, who were laughing noisily, and some middle-aged French people making loud jokes. Some West Germans – only Western currencies were accepted – were singing in chorus. A jazz record was playing, but could scarcely be heard. Still, it was pleasant to rediscover the taste of whisky, the taste of evenings in Paris with André, with Philippe. (It was hot there: they would have sat on a café terrace in Montparnasse.)

'Are you pleased to find yourself back in the West?'

'For a while, yes.'

André had burned his bridges. He had written to no one, having scribbled the briefest of notes on Nicole's last letter to Philippe. He smiled in the mornings when she stubbornly bought a copy of *Humanité* which was several days old. He was always the same on trips. He easily forgot Paris; he did not have his roots there.

'Partying conference delegates are worse than a wig-maker's wedding!' he said glumly.

'Do you want us to leave?'

'Of course not.'

He was staying to please Nicole; but he would not want to come back. And neither would Macha, who was ill at ease. (There were no Russians there, apart from two heavily made-up women, who were obviously trying their luck.) Yet it was a pleasant spot that opened out into the world beyond or at least gave a glimpse of it. A tall black man, in a red shirt, had started dancing all on his own, and people were marking the rhythm by clapping their hands.

'He dances really well,' said Nicole.

'Yes.'

André seemed absent. He had contracted a habit some days ago: he pressed a finger against his cheek, at the level of his gums. She said, a little impatiently:

'Are you in pain? Go to see a dentist.'

'I'm not in pain.'

'Then why are you fingering your cheek all the time?'

'I'm making sure that it's not painful.'

He had had a phase when he took his pulse twenty

times a day, staring rigidly at the hands of his watch. Little compulsions that are not serious, but which constitute a sign, nevertheless. Of what? That life is grinding to a halt, that senility is around the corner. Senility – she knew the Larousse definitions by heart: their asymmetry had struck her. Youthfulness: the quality of being youthful. Senility: weakening of the body and mind brought on by old age.

Youri and Nicole had left immediately after lunch. André had stayed with Macha for his Russian lesson. He reached for the small carafe of vodka: 'Enough work for today.' He added disappointedly: 'I've lost my memory.'

'Not at all; you do very well.'

'I don't retain what I learn. I forget as I'm going along.'

He drank a mouthful of vodka and Macha shook her head disapprovingly: 'I'll never get used to that way of drinking.'

She emptied her glass in a single swallow.

'It's true that one month is a derisory amount of time for learning a language,' he said.

'Why one month? You have nothing special to do in Paris, do you?'

'Nothing.'

'Well then, stay a little longer.'

Why not? I'll talk to Nicole about it this evening. On fine summer days like this, Moscow was very gay. People were pressing around the street vendors selling kvass and beer on tap; they were besieging the automatic machines which, for one kopeck, cough up more or less fresh water, and, for three kopecks, soda with a vaguely fruity taste. Their faces expressed good humour. They were much less disciplined than André had imagined; they crossed the roads when the traffic lights were at red, just as calmly as they did when they were at green. He thought back to the conversation he had had at lunch with Youri.

'Youri didn't convince me,' he said.

'Yet I can assure you that he's right,' said Macha.

They had been talking about the agreements recently reached with Renault, and André had been astonished that the USSR envisaged making 600,000 individual cars rather than improving its road network and public transportation. But public transportation worked well, said Youri; and building roads before the population felt the need, would be an inept policy: people would clamour for roads themselves when they had cars. Even under a socialist regime, citizens have the right to certain satisfactions of a private kind. The government was making strong efforts to develop consumer goods; they were to be congratulated for it.

'Do you think that you will succeed in building socialism by making more and more concessions to private property?'

'I think that socialism is made for men and not the opposite,' she said.

'One has to give a little thought to their short-term interests.'

'Yes, of course.'

What had he imagined exactly? That people's interests here were different?

That they were less attached to material goods?

That the socialist ideal remained alive in them and replaced everything else for them?

'The Chinese accuse us of losing ground; it's absurd. There's no question of going back to capitalism. But you must realise that this people has had only a life of sacrifices: during the war, and during the period of reconstruction. Even now, we are hardly spoiled. We can't have this austerity imposed upon us indefinitely.'

'What you call "austerity" doesn't seem so striking to me. My own childhood was harder than Vassili's. My mother's life hasn't been easy. She is happy – at least, as far as one can be at 83 – but that's because she has so few needs.'

'Why do you say "as far as one can be at 83"? It must be

very satisfying to feel that you have a long and very full life behind you.'

She was deliberately diverting the conversation.

She did not like talking to André about this country, which she considered to be her own: whether he criticised or praised the USSR, she was rather impatient with him.

'You look at things too abstractly,' she often said.

He dropped the topic.

'At 83, you don't have any future; and that takes all the charm away from the present.'

'If I live that long myself, I think I shall spend my time telling myself the story of my life. It's wonderful to have 83 years behind you! Think of all the things she has seen!'

'Even I have seen a fair number of things. But what's left of them for me?'

'A very great deal, of course. Everything you were telling me yesterday about your period with the Red Falcons, about the electoral bust-ups in Avignon . . .'

'I can tell people, but I don't really remember.' It would be fine, he often thought, if the past were a landscape in which one could wander at will, discovering little by little how routes meander and double back. But this was not so. He could recite names and dates, in the way that a schoolboy recites a well-learned lesson. He had a certain knowledge, and some distorted, faded images, as static as those in an old history book – they sprang up, at random, against a blank background.

'All the same, getting older is enriching,' said Macha. 'I feel more enriched now than when I was twenty. Don't you?'

'A little richer; but also much less so.'

'What is it that you've lost?'

'Youth.'

He poured himself a glass of vodka. His third? Or his fourth?

'I hated being young myself,' she said.

He stared at her rather remorsefully. He had created her, then abandoned her to a stupid mother and to an ambassador.

'Did you miss having a real father?'

She hesitated: 'Not consciously. I was concerned with the future. With escaping from my surroundings. Making my marriage a success. Bringing Vassili up properly. Making myself useful. And then, as I became more mature, I felt the need – how can I put it? – for roots. The past has become important: that is, France. And you.'

She looked at him in a trusting way, and he felt guilty; not just because of the past, but because at that moment he would have liked to offer her someone more brilliant as a father.

'Aren't you a little disappointed that I have dried up?'

'Of course not! For one thing, you still have plenty of time in front of you.'

'No. It's clear that I shall never produce anything else. Perhaps it might just be possible if I left Paris. But Nicole couldn't put up with living anywhere else. Or with being further away from Philippe.'

He had talked about it once, jokingly. And she had replied, jokingly: 'You would die of boredom as much as I would.' No, he often thought of it longingly. His mother's presence did not weigh heavily: she would not have been a nuisance to them. He would have done some gardening, fished for trout in the green waters of the Gard, walked in the scrubland with Nicole, done some reading, lazed about, and perhaps done some work. Perhaps. But, in any case, that was his only chance. It would never happen in Paris.

'In any case, it doesn't matter much,' she said.

'I'm of the same opinion as Nicole: you should live in the way you want.'

'I'm not sure that that's what she really thinks. And you yourself said that it's a pity!'

'It was just for something to say.' She bent over and kissed him.

'I love you the way you are.'

'And what way is that?'

She smiled: 'Are you looking for compliments? Well, what struck me in 1960 – and it remains true – is how you could give yourself to others, and at the same time, be present to yourself. And then the attention that you pay to things: when I'm with you, everything becomes important. And you are bright and cheerful. And I swear that you have stayed young: younger than all the people I know. You've lost nothing.'

'Well, if you're pleased with me like that . . .'

He smiled, too, but he knew very well that he had lost something: the fire, the sap that the Italians have such a nice name for: stamina. He emptied his glass. That was probably why he sought the joyful warmth of alcohol. Too much so, Nicole said. But what else is left for us, at our age? He touched his gum. It was scarcely sensitive. But a little, nevertheless. If the dentist did not manage to save the tooth that was supporting his bridge, there would be no other solution than dentures. How dreadful! He no longer wanted to be attractive: but at least he wanted people to be able to imagine, on looking at him, that he had been attractive. If only he could avoid becoming an entirely sexless being. When he was scarcely beginning to get used to his condition as an adult, he was going to be thrust into that of a very old man.

No!

'Does Nicole feel badly about growing old, too?'

'Less than I do, I think.'

'Was she disappointed not to go to Rostov?'

'A little.'

The irrepressible Nicole, he thought affectionately. As energetic and eager as she was at twenty. Without her, he would have been content to wander around the Moscow streets, chatting about this and that, sitting down on benches. Perhaps in that way he would have absorbed the atmosphere of the city better. But if he had told her that, it would have hurt her, and he did not want that for anything in the world.

'Five o'clock! And she's expecting us at five,' said Macha. 'We must hurry.'

They left the apartment in a rush. Nicole liked Macha's apartment very much. The courtyard was sad, the staircase dingy, the rusty metal elevator was often stuck, but the three small rooms – one for each of them, plus a kitchen and a bathroom – had been very well arranged, with a few photos, some well-chosen reproductions, fine carpets that Youri had brought back from Asia, and some objects collected by Macha during her childhood travels. As she went down the staircase, Nicole was suddenly nostalgic for her own studio apartment, her furniture, her own objects. It came back to her as it was when she had left it on the last morning, with a large bouquet of roses on her table, as young and fresh as young lettuce. You never saw roses here. And since her arrival – ten days ago – she had heard no music: it was almost a physical privation. She turned the corner of the road onto the big avenue that led to the hotel. In Paris, she knew all the shops on Boulevard Raspail; the faces of many people were familiar to her, and they all spoke to her. These faces meant nothing to her. Why was she so far away from her own life? It was a fine June day. The trees were in heat; the pigeons were flapping about in the pools of soft, fleecy pollen lying on the pavements, and its white flakes were fluttering down around Nicole, getting into her nose and mouth, sticking to her hair, making her head spin. They were fluttering down into the library and sticking to her hair on that afternoon when she had, in a certain way, said goodbye to her body. There had already been signs before that. In the mirror, in photographs, her image had come to look worn, but she still recognised herself in it.

When she was chatting with male friends, they were men and she felt herself to be a woman. And then this young man that she did not know – he was so handsome – had arrived with André. He had shaken her hand with a kind of distracted politeness and something had definitively been undermined. For her, he was a young, attractive male: for him, she was as asexual as an eighty-year-old woman. She had never recovered from that look; she had stopped coinciding with her body, which was now an unfamiliar skin, a kind of distressing disguise. Perhaps the metamorphosis had taken rather longer than that, but her memory crystallised it in that image: two doe eyes turning away from her with indifference. From that point on, she had remained unresponsive in bed: you have to like yourself a little to take pleasure in being in someone's arms. André had not understood her, but little by little he had allowed himself to be defeated by her coldness. The memory came back to her every summer, on this very same date, but she had stopped being wounded by it long ago. She usually took in good spirit this vague, springtime nostalgia that the dance of the pollen awakened in her, seeing it as a reminder of a time when the beauty of each day contained promises for the future. But today she felt both tense and listless – ill at ease with herself.

'Why?' she asked herself when she arrived back in her room. She sat on the window ledge, watching the cars diving down into the tunnel only to reappear on the other side of Gorky Street: 'I think I'm a little bored,' she said to herself. She did not find Moscow particularly charming. Being a little bored isn't a serious matter. They were going to leave for Leningrad; they would see Pskoff and Novgorod. She picked up a book. Normally, to be rid of her morose thoughts, she had only to explain them to herself, but the word 'bored' had solved nothing – she was still ill at ease. 'This is a sad room,' she told herself. 'Sad room,' what does that mean? When Philippe had told her that he was getting married, the bright harmony of the colours of the cushions, the charm of the hyacinths, the fine Nicolas de Staël reproduction had not helped her. All the same, at neutral moments like this, a joyful colour, an elegant shape, an agreeable object can be enough to revive your taste for life. Here nothing did so. Neither what was happening in the streets, nor the walls, nor the furniture consoled her. Consoled her over what? 'It's André!' she suddenly said to herself. 'I see him all the time, yet I never see him.' In 1963, Macha was preoccupied with her work: this year she was with them every single minute. For her, that was natural. But didn't André ever want to be alone with Nicole? Had he changed so much? In the past, a very, very long time ago, he was the more passionate one. At that stage she was not ready for passion. To be ready for it you have to be lacking something, to be torn, or to have something to compensate for: in André's case, it was his tough childhood, his mother's austerity, the failure of his love life with Claire. But in her own case it was the opposite: her parents had pampered her, and love was not the most important thing in her life; she wanted to become someone. She was the one who, after sex, left the bed first. He would try to keep holding her against him, murmuring: 'Don't go away: it's like being weaned.' (She often gave in, a little grudgingly.) And then, throughout their long life together, her need for him and the joy that he brought her had done nothing but grow. Now it was impossible to say which of the two of them was fonder of the other. Linked like Siamese twins: he is my life, and I am his. And yet there it was: it was not hurting him to never see her alone. Had his feelings cooled down? Sometimes indifference comes over people as they grow old: he had not been as upset by the death of his sister as he was earlier by his father's. Should she talk to him about it? Perhaps that would make him sad. She put her book down and stretched out on her bed. Too much for lunch, too much vodka – sleep was overcoming her.

'Where am I? Who am I?' Every morning, even before she opened her eyes, she recognised her bed and her room. But sometimes, when she slept in the afternoon, she experienced this infantile bewilderment when she woke up: Why am I who I am? As if her consciousness, emerging anonymously from the darkness, was hesitating before taking on an incarnation again. What surprised her – as it does the child when he becomes aware of his own identity – was finding herself back at the heart of her own life and not of a different one: by what stroke of fate? She might not have been born: then the question would not have arisen. 'I could have been someone else, but then it would be someone else questioning herself about her self.' It gave her vertigo to sense at once her contingency and the necessary coincidence between herself and her history.

Nicole, sixty years old, a retired teacher. 'Retired' – she had difficulty in believing it. She remembered her first job, her first class, the dead leaves rustling under her feet during an autumn in the provinces. At that stage her retirement day – separated from her by a stretch of time almost twice as long as the time she had already lived – seemed as unreal to her as death itself. But it had arrived. Sometimes she thought nostalgically of the doorway that she would not pass through again, of the waxed corridors, of the sounds of children rushing about and laughing that she would never hear again. She had stepped across other lines, but less well-defined ones. This one was as firm as an iron curtain. 'I am on the other side.'

She got up and recombed her hair. She was certainly putting some weight back on. It was annoying not to have any scales. Half past five. Why was he still not back? He certainly knew that she hated waiting. She hated waiting, but, as soon as he was there, there was so much warmth in her heart that she forgot she had been waiting for him.

'We couldn't find a taxi. We walked.'

'It doesn't matter at all,' she said.

'We worked well,' André said.

'And you drank a few glasses of vodka.'

She invariably spotted the slight distortion of pronunciation, the faint delay in his movements which indicated that André had had a drink or two. They were not yet clearly perceptible signs; she called them 'advance signs'.

'You have advance signs,' she added.

'I drank a little vodka, but I'm showing no advance signs.'

She did not press the matter. It was always with a heavy heart that she played the spoilsport, but she feared for his health, since his blood pressure was a little too high.

Sometimes she would wake up with a start: 'He risks getting lung cancer; having a heart attack; a stroke.'

'Look,' said André, 'Perfect balance.'

He seized Macha by the waist and twirled her around while humming a waltz. It was strange to see him with another woman. Even though she had his eyes, his chin. Nicole sometimes forgot that Macha was his daughter.

André talked to her with the words and the charming smiles that he had found for Nicole when they were young. Little by little, she and André had come to adopt with each other the curt tones of friendship; their gestures were almost gruff ones. Whose fault was it? Mine, obviously, she thought rather regretfully. She had been too well brought up, too formal, almost inhibited. He was the one who had immediately decided that they would say 'tu' to each other, and sometimes the exuberance of his affection embarrassed her. Little by little, she had slipped back into her former reserved manner: it would have been ridiculous to be an old married couple playing at turtle doves. Nevertheless, she felt vaguely jealous of his complicity with Macha, and reproached herself for not managing to retain that affectionate freshness in her relations with André. Her original rigidity had taken over again: she had never entirely overcome it, because she had never entirely accepted her condition as a woman. (Yet no man could have helped her to adjust to it as much as André had.)

'Do you like dancing?' she asked Macha.

'I adore it – with a good dancer.'

'I've never been able to dance myself.'

'Really? Why?'

'Because it's the male dancer who leads: I was silly when I was young. After that, it was too late.'

'I like being led,' said Macha. 'It's restful.'

'Provided that you are led in the direction you want to go,' said Nicole, smiling sympathetically at her. It was rare for her to sympathise with a woman. With her female students, of course: they were children, adolescents, and one could hope that they would not be like their elders. But adults! The young ones were of Irène's type. They carried out their 'career as a woman' with an ostentatious zeal. As if it were a career! The older ones took Nicole back to her rebellious childhood; they reminded her of her mother. 'Girls can't do that.' She couldn't be an explorer, nor an aviator, nor a captain of an ocean-going ship. Just a girl. Memories of chiffon, organdy, my mother's excessively smooth hands, the soft texture of her arms, her perfume which used to cling to my skin. She dreamed of Nicole marrying someone rich, having pearls and furs. And so the struggle had begun. 'Girls can do that.' She had prolonged her studies, had sworn to confound the destiny set out for her: she would write a sensational thesis, hold a chair at the Sorbonne; she would prove that a woman's brain is as good as a man's. None of that had happened. She had been a student, and an activist in feminist movements. But like the others – those others that she did not like – she had allowed herself to be devoured by her husband, her son, her home. Macha certainly did not allow herself to be devoured by anyone. Yet she accepted her femininity comfortably: probably because she had been living since the age of fifteen in a country where women have no inferiority complex. It was clear that Macha felt inferior to no one.

'Who's taking whom to dinner, where, and at what time?' Nicole asked.

'I've reserved a table, for 7:30, at the Bakou,' said Macha. 'We have plenty of time for a little stroll beforehand. It's a good time of day.'

'Right, let's go for a stroll,' said Nicole.

She had left her morose thoughts behind. André had come here to see Macha: it was natural that he should make the most of her presence. She looked forward cheerfully to the evening that all three of them were going to spend together.

★

André found the hotel that they stayed at in Leningrad charming. Long corridors and pearl-grey doors opening onto them, with oval panes at the top framed by old-fashioned festoons and hung with silk curtains, which were pink, green or blue according to which floor you were on. In their room there was an alcove, hidden by a curtain, and endearing old furniture: a heavy desk of false marble, a black leather sofa, a table covered by a tablecloth with fringes. Chandeliers with crystal pendants lit up the dining room, where a young, semi-naked woman in marble was adjusting her dress with a naughty smile – or was she taking it off?

'The service is as slow as in Moscow!' said Nicole. 'Fortunately, the orchestra isn't too loud.'

'It's true that they take their time,' said André, watching a waiter going up to a sideboard: he put a glass down on it and stayed gazing at it meditatively.

They all moved hesitantly and in a disorganised way, which was bound to exasperate clients who were in a hurry. The bricklayers and the labourers that one saw working in the street, the clerical workers, the shop assistants also looked nonchalant. And yet this country was not full of lazy people, otherwise they would not have been so extraordinarily successful in certain fields. The scientists and technicians probably had special training: they had a different mentality.

'Ah! Here comes the bill,' said Macha.

They left. How beautiful the light was at ten o'clock in the evening! At midday, the colours of the palaces were overwhelmed by the bright sunlight. But now, the blues, greens and reds throbbed gently in the fading sun.

'It's a wonderful city,' said Nicole.

Wonderful. The grace and splendour of the Italian baroque behind a Nordic glaze. And what gaiety along the banks of the bluish-white Neva river! It was mostly young people walking around in groups singing.

'All the same, you want to go to Pskoff and Novgorod?'

'There's time to do everything,' said Macha.

No doubt, but for his own part he would have liked to stay here for ten days. Leningrad, Petrograd, Saint-Petersburg. He would have liked to grasp everything about them, and even – though it was an impossible dream – to grasp everything at the same time. The city besieged one winter's day, with men and women staggering in the snow, and falling over never to get up again; the corpses being dragged across the frozen ground. The corpses strewn over Nevsky Prospekt; the men running; the bullets whistling past; the sailors attacking the Winter Palace. Lenin.

Trotsky. Was there not a way to conjure up the great saga that took place during his adolescence and somehow have it superimposed? It seemed so far away then, but so close now, as he trampled over the very places where it had unfolded. The setting had remained, but it did not help to bring the men and the events back to life. Quite the contrary. Historians were partly successful in reviving them, but to follow it all you had to abandon the world of the present, shut yourself up in the silence of your study, alone in front of your book. In these streets the density and weight of reality suppressed the mirages of the past: it was impossible to inscribe them in these stones. But, this evening, there was still Leningrad, on a clear and beautiful night. In 1963, they had come in August; the sun was setting. Today it was not setting. There was a festival. Along the river banks, boys and girls were dancing to the sound of a guitar. Others were sitting and playing the guitar on the benches of the Champ de Mars, to the rustle of lilac: luxuriant clusters of lilac, like those in French gardens, and Japanese lilac, growing more soberly and giving off a peppery scent. They sat down on a bench. Who were these boys with guitars? Students, office workers, manual workers? He gave up the idea of asking Macha. All too often she could not answer his questions and it bothered her. He was a little disappointed with her as a source of information. Perhaps people mistrusted her because of her foreign origins, or was society here as stratified as elsewhere? She knew nothing about working-class life, or peasant life, or the immense scientific and technical thrust that André would so much have liked some insights into.

'The first time I stayed up all night was when I was fifteen,' said Macha.

'I was overjoyed. I didn't understand how my parents could stay so calm. It's true that on that day I did think that it's terrible to grow old.'

'You don't think so any more?' said Nicole.

'I'm much more at ease with myself than I've ever been,' said Macha.

'Why, do you miss your youth?'

'No,' said Nicole. She smiled at André: 'As long as other people are growing old at the same time.'

The first time I stayed up all night, André repeated to himself. He became uneasy: this beautiful night of happiness did not belong to him. He could only take part in it: it was not his own. They were laughing and singing: he felt excluded, a tourist. He had never liked being in this position. But then again, in countries where tourism is a national industry, travelling around is a way of being integrated into them. On Italian café terraces, or in London pubs, he was one consumer among others; an espresso coffee tasted the same in his mouth as it did in that of someone from Rome. Here he would have had to get to know people through their work, to work with them. He was excluded from their leisure pursuits because he was excluded from their activities in general. An idler. No one else in the garden was an idler – just Nicole and himself.

And no one else was as old as they were. How young everyone was! He had been young. He could remember the ardent and sweet flavour that life had at that time: this night had it for them, too; they were smiling at the future. What was the present without a future, even amidst the scent of lilac and in the freshness of dawn experienced at midnight? For a moment, he thought: it's a dream, I'm going to wake up, I'll have my body back, I'm twenty. No. He was an adult, an aging man, almost an old man. He looked at them with envious stupefaction: why am I no longer one of them? How could this have happened to me?

They walked back from the Hermitage, where they had spent two hours: their third visit this year. They had seen again everything that they wanted to see for a second time. They were leaving the following day for Pskoff; they would visit Pushkin's property. Macha said the countryside was very beautiful and Nicole was delighted at the idea of smelling grass again. Leningrad was a very beautiful city, but you stifled in it. She took the key held out by the floor supervisor, who also gave Macha a note: the Intourist office wanted to see her urgently. 'There'll be some more complications,' said Nicole.

'It's probably a matter of settling a few details,' said André.

His incurable optimism! He buried himself in his Russian grammar and she opened her copy of *Humanité*. She was longing for the car journey, countryside, fresh air, some novelty. She knew the Hermitage, Smolny, the palaces, the canals by heart; she did not want to spend another three days here.

Macha came through the door: 'Permission refused!' she said, in a furious voice.

'I saw it coming,' Nicole said to herself gloomily.

'I did battle with the guy at Intourist, but he can't do anything; he has received orders. It's exasperating. They're exasperating.'

'Who are "they"?' André asked.

'I don't know exactly. He wouldn't tell me anything. Perhaps there are troop movements. But there's probably nothing at all.'

The panic that Nicole felt welling up inside her was disproportionate. Her impatience at the slightest obstacle, the fear of being bored — it was becoming neurotic. Come on now. What if they left tomorrow for Novgorod? But there wouldn't be hotel rooms available; everything always had to be arranged in advance. And then the stay in Moscow would be interminable in that case. Quickly, think of something else.

'And what about that trip you had talked about, the monastery on an island?'

'That will be forbidden, too.'

'You can always try.'

'Oh, no!' said André. 'She mustn't start all over again, going through those annoying hoops only to be told "No" once more. Let's just stay here quietly. To tell you the truth, I don't want to see that monastery.'

'Fine. Let's not talk about it any more,' said Nicole.

As soon as they had left her, she gave in to her anger. 'Three days of boredom here!' Suddenly, everything seemed boring to her: the straight avenues, the monotonous streets, the interminable dinners with music playing, the hotel room, the whole life here and the endless discussions between Macha and André: he defended the Chinese, whom she hated and feared; he criticised the policy of co-existence at any price which she supported. They kept going over the same ground. Or else André would tell Macha stories that Nicole knew by heart. She was still never seeing him on his own, or, at least, only for moments too brief to get a conversation going: he threw himself into a Russian book and she into a newspaper . . . She leaned her forehead against the window. How ugly that huge ochre and black church was! 'Permission refused.' If at least she could have discussed it, argued.

But everything rested on Macha's shoulders, and perhaps she was too easily discouraged. The dependency was irritating. Nicole had been amused by it at the beginning, but now it weighed on her. In Paris, she stood at the centre of her own life, making the decisions herself, with André or alone.

Here the initiatives and ideas fell to someone else; she was just one element in Macha's universe. She looked at her books; she had not brought enough, and those that really interested her she had read in Moscow. She went back to the window. The square and the little public garden, the people sitting on benches – everything seemed dull in the flat afternoon light. Time was stagnating. It's terrible – she wanted to say: it's unfair – that time can pass so fast and so slowly at the same time. She was going through the front door of the lycée in Bourg, almost as young as her pupils; she was looking pityingly at the old teachers with grey hair. And, then presto, she had been an old teacher and then the lycée door had closed behind her! For years, her classes of pupils had given her the illusion that her own age was not changing: with each new year she met up with them again, as young as ever, and she believed she was unchanging too. In the ocean of time, she was a rock battered by new waves all the time, but unmoving and not being worn down. And now the tide was carrying her along, would carry her along onto the beach of her death. Tragically, her life was slipping by. And yet it was running out in drips, hour by hour, minute by minute. You always had to wait for the sugar to dissolve, for the memory to subside, for the wound to heal, for the boredom to dissipate. A strange fracture between these two rhythms. My days are galloping past, but each day I languish.

She turned away from the window. What a void there was inside her, all around her, as far as she could see. During the last year she had helped Philippe with his research. At the stage he had reached, she could be of no further use to him. And he lived elsewhere. Reading at random, with no specific purpose, was a way of passing the time that was scarcely more interesting than doing crosswords or playing

'Spot the Mistakes'. She had told herself: 'I shall have time, all my time to myself. What a stroke of fortune!' It is not a stroke of fortune if you find nothing to do with your time. It is even the case, she had realised, that too much leisure impoverishes you. It was on leaving home early in the morning or on coming out of the subway that she would sometimes be struck – in the old days – by the violent, unexpected pleasure afforded by light reflecting on a tiled roof, or the colour of a certain sky. While she was walking slowly through the streets, open to experiences, it eluded her. You sense the brightness of the sun much better when it is filtered through closed shutters than when you are faced directly with its torrid harshness. She had never been able to put up with boredom. And if she was suffering from it to the point of anguish this afternoon, it was because it was overflowing into her future. Years of boredom, until death finally ensued. 'If only I had projects, if only I were engaged in some work!' she told herself.

Too late. She should have gotten started on something earlier; it was her own fault. Not only her fault. André had not helped her. He had put pressure on her, in an insidious way: 'You've worked enough; don't do any more correcting; come to bed . . . Stay in bed a little while longer . . . Come for a walk . . . I'll take you to the cinema.' He had crushed all of Nicole's vague desires, without even being aware of it. 'All I had to do was not to give in to him,' she told herself. She was inventing certain resentments. But that was because she resented what André had done. He had made a decision, without even discussing things with her: 'Let's just stay here!' And above all, above all he was not making the least effort to keep Macha at a slight distance; the idea did not even occur to him. Is he less fond of me? In Paris, we are bound together by a network of habits so tight that it leaves no room for any questions. But beneath that shell what remains between us that is living and true? Knowing what he is to me does not tell me what I am for him. 'I'll talk to him,' she decided. In Moscow. Macha had plenty to do; they were not obliged to keep her with them all the time. And yet what was the good of arranging tête-à-tête sessions with him if he did not spontaneously want them? No. She would not talk to him. She began writing a letter to Philippe.

'Now, this is a functioning church. Do you want to go in?' Macha said.

'Of course,' said Nicole. 'Oh, what a beautiful golden light!'

On the walls, on the icon screen, the icons gently glowed, and even the shadows were like flowing gold. But the smells made André feel sick: the scent of incense, of candles, and the smell of the poor old women on their knees on the floor, mumbling, grovelling and kissing the slabs. It was even more offensive than in Catholic churches. A nasal voice rose from the back, on the left. They went closer. What a strange sight. Men and women – young men and women – were moving in circles around an orthodox priest with a long silky black beard, attired in his finery – all of them holding in their arms babies dressed in white, who were crying. The priest was sprinkling the infants from a holy water sprinkler while chanting prayers. It seemed like a game, with the parents rocking their bawling children and going round in circles.

'Assembly-line baptism! I'd never seen that before,' said Macha.

'Do parents often have their children baptised?'

'When they have an old mother who is a believer and don't want to hurt her.'

'And what's going on over there?' said Nicole.

There were boxes lined up against the walls: empty coffins. And six had been placed on the floor side by side, each with a dead body in it: the exposed faces, waxen and framed by chinstraps, were all alike.

'Let's leave,' Nicole said.

'Does this disturb you?'

'Rather. Doesn't it disturb you?'

'No.'

He looked upon his own death with indifference: surviving, surviving one's death seemed to him more arduous than dying. The death of others . . .

He had become hardened. At 25, he had sobbed when he had lost his father. And then two years ago, he had buried his sister without shedding any tears, although he had loved her very much. And his mother? Macha thought of her at the same time as he did.

'I'd very much like to see my grandmother before she dies,' she said.

'Will it hurt you when she dies?'

He hesitated: 'I don't know.'

'But you adore her!' said Nicole, in a surprised tone. 'It will certainly hurt me,' she said.

'And then it will have a strange effect on me. There will be no one left from the generation before ours. That will push us back one notch further.'

They went back to the Nevsky Prospekt by taxi, and sat down in an open-air café. He ordered a cognac: it was not very good, but they did not serve vodka in cafés. Cognac was much more expensive, to discourage drunks.

In practice, a lot of people came along with a bottle of vodka in their pocket.

'Are there many religious funerals?'

'No. There, too, it's mostly old women who ask to be buried by the church or bring their dead to the church.' Macha hesitated: 'All the same, I went into a Moscow church one Sunday morning and I was astonished. There were quite a few men, of early middle age, or even young. Many more than there used to be.'

'It's regrettable,' said André.

'Yes.'

'If people want to believe in heaven, it's because they don't believe in much on earth any more. It means that the policy of material well-being that you are beginning to pursue here is not as successful as you say.'

'Oh, well-being! Let's not exaggerate,' said Macha. 'I've never denied that ideologically we are currently in a period when we are slipping back,' she added.

'A period that will last how long?'

'I don't know. There are young men like Vassili and his comrades who are full of enthusiasm. They will fight for a socialism that excludes neither happiness nor freedom.'

'It's a fine programme,' said André sceptically.

'You don't believe in it?'

'I wouldn't say that. But in any case I won't see that kind of socialism myself.'

Yes, his discomfort had a name, a name that he did not like but was obliged to use: disappointment. In general, he detested the travellers who came back from China, from Cuba, from the USSR, or even from the USA saying: I was disappointed. They had been wrong to have a priori ideas which the facts subsequently refuted; it was their fault and not the fault of reality. But, in the end, it was something analogous that he himself experienced. Perhaps things would have been different if he had visited the virgin lands of Siberia, or the towns where the scientists were working. But in Moscow and in Leningrad, he did not find what he had been hoping for. What had he been hoping for exactly? It was vague. In any case, he had not found it. Of course, there was a great difference between the USSR and the West. Whereas in France technical progress only deepened the divide between privileged people and those being exploited, here the economic structures were in place to ensure that one day technical progress would benefit everyone. Socialism would end up by becoming a reality. One day it would triumph in the whole world. This was just a matter of a period when things were slipping back. In the whole world – except perhaps in China, but what one knew about that country was uncertain and scarcely reassuring – countries were going through a period when things were slipping back. Admittedly, they would come out of it. That was possible, that was probable. A probability that André himself would never verify. For young people, this moment was no worse than any other, no worse than the period when he was twenty: only, these years which for them were a point of departure represented a terminal point for him, a fall.

At his age, he would not witness the revival that was perhaps to follow. The road leading to the good is worse than evil itself, says Marx. When you are young, with an illusory eternity in front of you, you jump to the end of the road in one leap; later, you do not have enough strength to surpass what have been called the incidental casualties of history, and you consider them to be appallingly high. He had counted on history to justify his life: he was not counting on it any longer.

All things considered, the time had passed quite quickly. Two pleasant days in Novgorod; and in less than a week she would rediscover Paris, her house, her life, and André. He smiled at her: 'You wanted to go into a dacha. Well, it's been arranged,' he said.

'How kind Macha is!'

'It's a friend's dacha, about thirty kilometres away. Youri will drive us there, not this Sunday, but the one after.'

'The one after? But we're leaving on Tuesday.'

'Of course not, Nicole: you know very well that we decided to stay for ten days longer.'

'You decided that, without saying a single word to me!' said Nicole.

Suddenly, there was a red mist in her head, a red fog in front of her eyes, something red shouting out in her throat. He couldn't care less about me! Not a single word!

'But, look, I did; I talked to you about it. I would never have made the decision without talking to you about it. You agreed.'

'You're lying!'

'It was on the day I had drunk a little vodka at Macha's apartment, and when you claimed that I had advance signs. We had dinner at the Bakou. When we got back, when we were alone, I talked to you about it.'

'You said nothing, ever. You know very well. I can assure you that I would have noted the occasion. You decided without me and now you're lying.'

'You've forgotten. Come on, have I ever faced you with a fait accompli?'

'There's a first time for everything. And you're lying, into the bargain. It's not the first time that that's happened.'

In the past, he never used to lie. But this year, he had lied over little things, twice. He had laughed, and excused himself: 'It's my age; you become lazy. It would have taken too long to explain myself, so I took a shortcut.' He had promised not to do it again. He was doing it again. And this time it was more serious than a matter of an empty bottle, of a visit to the doctor that he had skipped. Her anger: only rarely – very rarely – had she been angry with André. But then it was a tornado that carried her thousands of kilometres away from him; and from herself, out of her life, out of her skin, into a horrible solitude that was both glacial and scorching . . . He looked at her changed, stubborn face, her tight lips; the face that used to frighten him so much, and which still moved him deeply. I told her, and she has forgotten. At that point, she was still enjoying herself here: ten days more, or less, were of no great significance. She had begun to be bored little by little. She missed Philippe. I'm not enough for her; I've never been enough for her. I told her in this room, after our dinner at the Bakou. But like all the people who think they have an infallible memory, she wouldn't admit that she could ever be mistaken. Just the same, she knew very well that he decided nothing without consulting her; and during this trip he had done every single thing that she wanted. An extra ten days in Moscow, it wasn't an enormous thing to swallow.

'Listen, there's nothing dreadful about ten extra days here.'

Nicole's eyes were sparkling with rage, one might almost have said with hatred.

'I'm bored! You're not aware of how bored I am!'

'Oh, I'm aware of it! You miss Philippe, and your friends. I know very well that I have never been enough for you.'

'Go away, leave me alone. I can't bear seeing you any more. Go away.'

'What about Youri and Macha? They're waiting for us downstairs.'

'Tell them I have a headache. Tell them whatever you like.'

He closed the door, agitated. 'That's how bored she is with me!' She had not even protested when he had said to her: 'I have never been enough for you.' He was not so eager to stay, but Macha was counting on it, and he did not want to hurt her. Nicole should have understood . . . But he lost heart at the idea of quarrelling with her. He found any disagreement between them unbearable. Anyway, he would come back straight after dinner; she would surely agree to listen to him. Was there any chance that he really had neglected to talk to her about it? No, he could see himself sitting down on his bed in his pyjamas, while she was brushing her hair. What had she replied? 'Why not?' or something of that kind. I never decide anything without her, she knows that very well. As soon as the door closed, tears suffocated her. As if, although he was still alive, she had lost André for ever. In less than a minute the guillotine can cut a head off; in less than a minute an utterance had cut off her links with André. How could she have imagined that they were welded to each other? Because of their past, she took for granted that he was as attached to her as she to him. But people change; he had changed. The fact that he lied was not the worst thing: he was lying out of cowardice, like a child who is afraid of being scolded. The worst thing was that he had made the decision with Macha, without taking her into account; that he had completely forgotten her, neglecting to consult her, or even to warn her. She needed the courage to face up to things: in three weeks he has never tried to arrange a tête-à-tête between us. All his smiling, all his affection is for Macha; he doesn't care what I want and don't want. 'Let's stay in Moscow then. Let's stay in Leningrad.'

He enjoyed being here. He took it for granted that she enjoyed it, too. It's not love any more: I am just a habit.

She could not bear to be in the room any longer. She tidied her face up and went down into the street. Walk: she had often walked in order to calm her fears, fits of anger; to get rid of images. Only, she was not twenty any more, or even fifty; she very quickly became tired. She sat down on a bench in a little public garden, opposite a pond where a swan was gliding. People stared at her as they went by; she must look dazed; or perhaps they simply recognised her as a foreigner. He was probably dining with Youri and Macha, in the restaurant at the harbour station, beside the Moskva, as they had planned to do. Perhaps the evening had an unpleasant aftertaste for him, but even that was not sure, since he had the art of being caught up in the moment, of blocking out anything that bothered him. He was forgetting her, putting her to one side; he was telling himself that she would have calmed down when he came back. He had always been that way: as soon as he was happy, she must be too. In fact, there had been no real symmetry between their two lives. He had had exactly what he wanted: a home, children, leisure, pleasures, friendships and a little turbulence. Whereas she had given up all her youthful ambitions – because of him. He had never wanted to recognise that. It was because of him that she had become this woman who no longer knew how to spend the time that she had left to live. Someone else would have pressed her to work, would have preached by example. He had turned her away from work. Now she found herself empty-handed, having nothing in the world but him, and suddenly she didn't have him. There was an atrocious contradiction in an anger born out of love that kills love. With every second, as she conjured up André's face and voice, she stoked up a grudge which was devastating her. It was like those illnesses where you forge your own suffering; each time you breathe in, it tears at your lungs, and yet you are obliged to breathe. 'What's to be done, then?' she asked herself in a stupor as she returned towards the hotel. There was no way out. They would continue to live together, she would bury her grievances; many couples vegetate in this way, in a state of resignation, of compromise. In a state of solitude. I am alone. Next to André, I am alone. I must convince myself of that.

She opened the door of their room. On the bed were André's pyjamas; his slippers were on the floor, a pipe and a packet of tobacco on the night table. For a moment he existed poignantly for her, as if an illness or exile had taken him away from her and she were finding him again in these abandoned objects. Tears came to her eyes. She stiffened.

She took a tube of sleeping pills from her medicine bag, swallowed two tablets and went to bed.

'I'm alone!' She was stricken with anguish: the anguish of existing, something much more intolerable than the fear of dying. Alone like a rock in the middle of the desert, but condemned to be aware of her useless presence. Her whole body, knotted, clenched, was a silent scream. And then she let herself slip between the sheets and sank into sleep. When she woke up, in the morning, he was asleep, huddled up with his hand pressed against the wall. She looked away. No impulse pulled her towards him. Her heart was icy and dulled, like a disused chapel where there is no longer even the tiniest night light. The slippers, the pipe moved her no more: they did not evoke the presence of someone dear to her who was absent; they were just an extension of the unfamiliar person who lived in the same room as she did. 'Oh, I hate him!' she told herself, in despair. 'He has killed all of the love that I had for him!'

She was coming and going about in the room, silent and hostile. Often, when they were young, he had come up against that closed face. 'I don't accept . . . One must not . . .' At the time, such severity petrified him. He was older than she, but for a long time he had regarded all adults as elders. Today, she made him impatient: 'How long is she going to go on sulking at me?' She was exaggerating. He had done everything to ensure that she was happy during this trip. And during their whole life together. He was staying in Paris because of her . . . Even if she had forgotten their conversation, she should have given him a little credit. It was as if she had leapt at the opportunity.

What grudges was she harbouring? Did she regret not having a more brilliant husband? In that case, she did not really love him. If she had really loved him, she would not have been bored with him. At the beginning of their marriage, her lukewarmness had hurt him, but he told himself that the day would come . . . He had thought that the day had come. But it seemed not. He had expected only one compensation in old age: Philippe was getting married, and she was retired, so he would have Nicole all to himself. But if she did not love him, if he was not enough for her, if she persisted in her grievances, then this dream of their being alone together was entirely compromised. They would have the sad old age of people who only stay together because, after a certain age, they can't really separate. No, he couldn't believe it. Were they one and the same woman, the one whose smile, even yesterday, radiated affection, and the one with her lips tightened in a furious pout?

'How furious you look!'

She made no reply, and he was gripped by anger, too.

'You know, if you want to leave before me, I'm not stopping you.'

'That's exactly what I intend to do.'

He was shocked: he had not thought that she would take his offer seriously. Well, let her leave! he said to himself. At least, I know where things stand. I can't delude myself any more; I'm an old habit for her, but she has never truly loved me. I knew that once and then I forgot it. I must remember it. Harden my heart. Let her do what she wants. And I'll do what I want. He thought of the garden at Villeneuve, the smell of cypress trees and roses in the sweltering sun. When I get back from Moscow, I'll leave Paris. I'll set myself up in Provence: I've been too stupid, sacrificing myself for her. It's every man for himself.

Is it true what they claim then, that we can't communicate, that no one understands anyone else? Nicole asked herself. She looked at André, sitting on Macha's couch, with a glass of vodka in his hand, and she thought that she would have to revise their whole past. They had lived juxtaposed, every man for himself, not knowing each other, neither merged nor transparent. Just before leaving their room, in the morning, André had looked at her hesitantly; he would have liked to embark on an explanation. She had opened the door, he had followed her, and in the taxi they had both remained silent. There was nothing to explain. Words would be shattered against this anger, this pain, this stiffening of her heart. So much negligence, so much indifference!

In front of Macha, all day long they had played out a polite comedy. How can I announce to her that I'm leaving before André?

He was drinking a fourth glass of vodka; he was free to do so. When he was young, alcohol made him lyrical and charming: he went a little too far, but without becoming incoherent, or falling about. Now – since when? – both his words and his actions became tangled up, and the doctor had said that alcohol and tobacco were doing him no good; he was swallowing his own death in little mouthfuls. Again, fear – more corrosive than anger – made her stubborn. 'He drinks too much.' She pursed her lips. He was free. He could kill himself in small stages if that pleased him. In any case, they would both finish up by dying, and in certain cases that's just as good as living.

There was something senile about the way in which he tried to keep a conversation going in Russian with Macha. She was laughing at his accent; they were as thick as thieves.

From time to time he touched his cheek with his finger, in a preoccupied way. Nicole wanted to shout out: 'We're not so old, not yet, no!' He had changed; she had noticed it during this trip – perhaps because, although she never saw him, she was seeing him all of the time. He no longer wanted to just let himself live. Previously, living was the only thing he liked. But for him living was a process of perpetual invention, a joyful, unpredictable adventure in which he drew her along. Now he gave her the impression of vegetating: that's what old age is and I don't want it.

Something wavered in her mind. As it does when you have received a blow on the skull and vision is muddled; you see two images of the world, at two different levels, without being able to say what is above and what is below. The two images that she had of her life, of the past and of the present, could not be matched up. There was a mistake somewhere. This moment was a lie: it was not André and it was not Nicole; this scene was taking place somewhere else . . . No, alas! It was the past that was a mirage; that often happens. How many women are wrong about their lives, throughout their lives. Her own had not been the one that she used to tell herself. Because André was impetuous, emotional, she had thought that he cherished her passionately. In truth, he forgot her as soon as he could not see her. Third parties coming between them did not worry her. For her, André's presence was an inexhaustible joy, but hers was not for him. Perhaps I'm even a burden to him; perhaps I've always been a burden to him.

'Macha, we have to settle the question of my departure. You see, I have commitments in Paris.'

'Oh, let's not mince words!' said André. He turned towards his daughter: 'She's mad at me because she claims that I decided to extend our stay here without consulting her. In fact, as you can imagine, I talked to her about it.'

'Of course,' Macha said forcefully. 'The first thing that he said to me when I suggested that you should stay a little longer was: "I'll talk to Nicole about it."'

The complicity between them!

'He didn't do so. He forgot to do it, and he's lying to me.'

Again, she was giving herself the appearance of a Gorgon. But for the first time in his life she did not intimidate him. She was wrong, entirely wrong. Macha was trying to patch things up, but she was replying coldly, and watching him pour himself some vodka with blame in her eyes. A pain in the ass, that's what she's in the process of becoming. He defiantly swallowed the vodka in one gulp, Russian style.

'You can get drunk, it makes no difference to me,' she said in an icy voice.

'Please, please, don't go back to Paris so quickly; that depresses me,' said Macha.

'It may depress you, but it doesn't depress him.'

'No, it doesn't depress me.'

'You see. At least we're in agreement about that. He'll be able to down ten bottles of vodka without anyone protesting.'

'Really, it's not in the least amusing to see you pulling your long face. I think that a short separation will do us both good. When I get back from Moscow, I'll go down to Villeneuve. And I'm not asking you to follow me.'

'Rest assured, I won't follow you.'

She rose: 'We can't bear to see each other any more: let's not see each other any more.'

She walked towards the door. Macha took her arm: 'This is stupid. Come back. Talk things out between you.'

'Neither of us wants to.'

The door slammed.

'You should have stopped her from leaving,' said Macha.

'I tried to talk things out this morning; she doesn't want to listen. To hell with her!'

'It's true that you drink rather too much,' said Macha.

'Fine. Put this bottle away.'

She put the bottle away and came back to sit opposite André, looking perplexed.

'You had both drunk a fair amount at the Bakou. You may have forgotten to talk to her yet believe you did.'

'Or else she didn't register the conversation because, being slightly drunk, she fell asleep immediately afterward.'

'That's possible, too. But in any case you are both sincere [*de bonne foi*]; so why are you both angry?'

'I'm not questioning her sincerity myself. She is the one who claims that I'm lying. She has no right to do that.'

Macha smiled: 'I would never have imagined that you could squabble like that . . . like children.'

'When we're over sixty? But, just think, what are adults and even old people? Just children swollen out with age.'

It was precisely because of their age that this quarrel was so odious to him. Nicole was betraying the whole long period of mutual understanding behind them. If she doubted his sincerity, it must be that she had never entirely had confidence in him; that he had never completely had her respect. And then always keeping a watch on how many glasses he was drinking, so that she could have the pleasure of being a pain. He did not want to think about her any more.

'Pass me *Pravda* and let's get down to work.'

'Now?'

'I'm not drunk,' he said, a little aggressively.

He began translating an article. After a moment she got up.

'I'm going to telephone to see that Nicole got back safely.'

'Why shouldn't she have done?'

'Just that she seemed quite beside herself.'

'In any case, I won't speak to her.'

Nicole had not arrived back. Nor an hour later, at midnight. Or she had probably got back, but was not answering the phone.

'I'll come up with you,' said Macha when she stopped the car in front of the hotel. 'I want to be sure that she is there.'

The floor supervisor gave André his key. So Nicole was not there. The silence and the emptiness of the room brought his heart into his mouth. The taste and effects of the vodka had disappeared, and his anger with them.

'Where can she be?'

He did not like to imagine her wandering through the sleeping city, where all the cafés were closed.

'There's one place open and she may be there: the bar at the National Hotel.'

'Let's go there,' he said.

Nicole was sitting in front of a glass of whisky, with a slack mouth and a fixed stare.

André would have liked to take her by the shoulders and embrace her. But at the first word he said, her face would change, and harden. He went up to her and smiled shyly.

Her face changed, hardened.

'What are you doing here?'

She had been drinking: words were slurred in her mouth.

'We've come to fetch you in the car.'

He placed his hand lightly on her shoulder: 'Come on, let's have a drink together. Let's make up our differences.'

'No wish to. And I'll go back when I'm ready.'

'We'll wait for you,' he said.

'No. I'll walk back. Alone. I think it's a bit rich that you've pursued me all this way.'

'Let me take you back now,' said Macha.

'Please, do it for me. If you don't, we'll end up waiting until two o'clock, and I have to get up early tomorrow morning.'

Nicole hesitated. 'Fine. But I'm doing it for you. Just for you,' she said.

Light filtered through her eyelids. She kept them closed. Her head was heavy and she was as sad as could be. Why had she got drunk? She was ashamed.

As soon as she arrived back she had thrown her clothes all over the place and had collapsed. She had sunk into deep darkness; it was fluid and stifling, oily, and this morning she could scarcely emerge from it. She opened her eyes. He was sitting in an armchair at the foot of her bed; he was smiling and looking at her.

'Darling, we can't go on like this.'

Suddenly, it was André again. She recognised him: past and present were one single image. But the iron band remained around her chest. Her lips were trembling. Stiffen herself still more, go straight down to the bottom, drown herself in the deep darkness. Or try to catch hold of this hand held out for her. He was speaking, in an even, calming voice; she loved his voice. No one can be sure what they remember, he was saying. Perhaps he hadn't talked to her, but he was sincere when he maintained that he had. She was no longer sure of anything either. She made an effort.

'Perhaps you did talk to me after all, and I've forgotten. I'd be surprised, but it's not impossible.'

'In any case, there's no reason for us to be angry.'

She managed to smile: 'None,' she said.

He came up to her, put his arms around her shoulders, kissed her on the temple. She clutched him to her and, with her cheek against his jacket, she began to cry. The warm voluptuous feeling of tears running down her cheek. What a release! It's so tiring to detest someone you love. He was saying the old words: 'My little one, my darling . . .'

'I've been stupid.'

'But I've been thoughtless. I should have come back to the subject. I should have understood that you were bored.'

'Oh, I'm not as bored as that. I exaggerated.'

'I'm bored because I'm not seeing you on your own': the words would not pass her lips. It would have seemed like a reproach. Or a request. She rose and went into the bathroom.

'Listen,' he said when she came back into the room. 'If you want to leave before me, then do it. But if I went with you, Macha would be very hurt. She suggested yesterday evening that I should leave with you, but that wouldn't be a nice thing to do. I'd very much like you to stay,' he added.

'Of course, I'll stay,' she said.

· 93 ·

She was trapped. Deprived of her anger, disarmed, she would not have the strength to carry out the hostile, and unnecessary, act of leaving. What was waiting for her in Paris?

'I can tell you that I'm starting to find it a long time, too,' he said. 'Living as a tourist in Moscow isn't much fun all of the time.'

'Anyway, as you said, there's nothing dreadful about ten days here,' she said.

In the corridor, she took his arm. They were reconciled, but she felt the need to reassure herself of his presence.

In the darkness of the cinema, André secretly looked at Nicole's profile. Since their quarrel, two days earlier, she seemed a little sad. Or was he projecting his own sadness onto her? Things were not exactly the same between them as before. Perhaps she regretted having agreed to stay another ten days in Moscow? Or else he himself had been more deeply wounded than he had thought by what she had told him and her anger. He could not manage to become interested in the story of this woman pilot. His mind was dwelling on morose thoughts. How could Macha imagine that growing old was an enrichment! Many people think that. It's the years that give wines their bouquet, furniture its patina, men their experience and wisdom. The claim is that each moment is encompassed and justified by the following moment, which itself prepares a more successful future, with even failures finally recuperated. 'Each atom of silence provides the chance of a ripened fruit.' He had never fallen for that. But neither did he see life in the way Montaigne did, as a succession of deaths: the newborn baby is not the death of the embryo, nor the child the death of the newborn baby. He had never seen Nicole die and come back to life. He even rejected Fitzgerald's idea that 'Life is a process of deterioration.'

He did not have the body he had at twenty, his memory was fading a little, but he did not feel diminished. And Nicole certainly was not. Until very recently, he had been quite convinced that, at eighty, they would still be just like themselves. He did not believe that any more. His incurable optimism, which Nicole smiled at, was less robust than it used to be. There were those teeth that he spat out in his dreams, those dentures that threatened him; and, on the horizon, decrepitude. He had hoped that, at least, there would never be a decline in their love; it even seemed that Nicole would belong to him more when she was old. And now something between them was perhaps in the process of unravelling. How could one distinguish, in their actions and their words, between what was just a routine repetition of the past and what was new and alive? His own feelings for Nicole remained as young as they were at the very beginning. But what about hers? There were no words with which he could ask her the question.

'Pick out some books for yourself,' Macha said to Nicole.

Their anxiousness to entertain her was a little irritating. It was a good film yesterday, but this afternoon this story of a woman pilot was a real drag. She could read, of course; in fact, what else could she do? Macha was working on a translation, and André was trying to decipher *Pravda* with the aid of a dictionary. She examined the Pléiade volumes lined up on a stand. Novels, novellas, memoirs, short stories – she had read them all, or almost all. But apart from the texts that she had analysed in classes, what could she remember? She could not recall precisely a single episode of Manon Lescaut, which she had dissected sentence by sentence while studying for her degree. And yet she felt lazy at the idea of going back to those pages that she could not conjure up any more. Re-reading bored her. You remember things as you go along, or at least you have the illusion of doing so. You are deprived of what makes reading joyful: that free collaboration with the author that is almost a creation. She was still curious about her own times, and she kept up with the new books coming out. But what did these old books that had made her what she was, and would continue to be, have to say to her?

'Your only problem is what to choose from all these,' said André. 'It is a problem.'

She took a volume by Proust. Proust was different. She waited for the sentences that she knew by heart, and she recognised them with all the happiness that the narrator had in recognising the musical phrase by Vinteuil.

But today she was finding it hard to concentrate. She was thinking: it's not the same any more. She looked at André. What is a presence? There was their long history together, which finally came to die upon the nape of his neck, and she was as familiar with their history, and had forgotten as much of it, as in the case of the texts enclosed in these covers. In Paris, he was present, even when he was some kilometres away. And it was perhaps even in those moments when, leaning out of the window, she watched him going away that he existed in her heart in the most powerful and certain way: his silhouette diminished and disappeared at the corner of the street, marking out with each step the route along which he would come back – the apparently empty space was a force field which, irresistibly, would bring him back to her, as if to his natural place. That certainty was even more moving than a body of flesh and bone. Today André was there in person, at arm's length, but between them, invisible and impalpable, was a kind of insulating layer: a layer of silence. Was André aware of it? Probably not. He would have replied: 'Not at all: things are as they were before. What has changed?'

There had been quarrels in their life, but for serious reasons. When one or the other of them had had an affair; or over Philippe's education. They were real conflicts, resolved violently, but quickly and definitively. This time, it had been a swirl of smoke, smoke without fire; and, because of its very thinness, it had not quite dispersed. It had also to be admitted, she thought, that formerly there had been torrid reconciliations in bed: pointless grievances were burned away in the heat of desire, excitement, pleasure; they found themselves facing each other refreshed and joyful. Now, this recourse was lacking. As a result, Nicole kept thinking about things too much. She had been largely responsible for their disagreement: she had thought that he was lying. (Well, why had he lied to her before, even though it was over little things?) It was also his fault. He should have come back to the matter, instead of considering it settled in two minutes. She had been too mistrustful, but he had been negligent, and he remained so, since he was not really worried about what was going on in Nicole's head. Had he become unfeeling? In the midst of her anger, she had thought many unjust things about him. No, he was not senile. Vegetating, no. But perhaps less sensitive than before. Inevitably, since one gets worn down: so many wars, massacres, catastrophes, misfortunes, deaths. When Manon dies, will I cry myself? 'There will be no one left to call me: my dear child,' she told herself sadly. But that was a selfish thought. Would she regret not seeing Manon any more? She remained vulnerable with regard to André and Philippe. But other people? And at this moment she felt no warmth even towards Philippe or André.

A couple going on together because they have started: was that the future that awaited them? Friendship, affection, but no real reason for living together: is that how it would be? There had been real reasons to begin with. She who bridled as soon as a boy tried to assert the slightest superiority over her had been won over by a kind of ingenuousness on his part, a kind that she had never met in anyone else. She was disarmed by how dismayed he seemed when he sighed: 'You are quite wrong!'. Overprotected by her mother, neglected by her father, she had this wound within her: that of being a woman. The idea of one day lying down beneath a man revolted her. By his sensitivity and his tenderness, André had enabled her to become reconciled with her sex. She had accepted sexual pleasure with joy. After a few years, she had even wanted a child; and motherhood had fully satisfied her. Yes, she had really needed André and not someone else. And, for his part, why had he loved her when, because of her aggressiveness, people did not generally like her? Perhaps the harshness and severity of his mother, which he found hard to take, were at the same time necessary to him, and perhaps he had found them again in Nicole. She had helped him to become, more or less, an adult. In any case, she had always had the impression that no woman would have suited him better than she did. Was she mistaken? On her own side, would she have been more fulfilled [*pleinement accomplie*] with someone else? Pointless questions. The only problem was to know what remained between them now. She did not know. Macha was busy that afternoon; she had left Nicole and André in the hands of a taxi driver, to whom she had given detailed instructions. They got out of the car in a suburb, where they had already been three years earlier and which was a true village at the gates of Moscow. They climbed up a street lined with old *isbas*.

'Don't walk so quickly: I want to take photos,' said Nicole.

She had suddenly announced that it was a shame not to take home any photos of their trip, and had borrowed Youri's camera. She had scarcely ever taken any photos. He watched her lining up an *isba* in the viewfinder. 'It's because she's bored with me,' he thought. In the taxi, they had found nothing to say to each other. Yet there was no longer any problem between them: that was the saddest thing. Perhaps he had become boring. Even during their vacations in Villeneuve, they never saw each other as much as they did here: she was over-saturated with his presence. And because she was bored, she herself was not much fun either. She photographed a second *isba*, and a third. People who were sitting on their doorsteps, chatting in the sun, looked at her with annoyance: one of them said something that André did not understand, but which did not seem pleasant.

'I think that they don't like you taking these photos,' he said.

'Why?'

'These *isbas* are pretty, but they find them wretched and they suspect you, an evil foreigner, of wanting to take away images of their misery.'

'Fine, I'll stop,' she said.

They slipped back into silence. In the final analysis, he had been wrong to extend their stay. What good did it do him, even in relation to Macha? They were going to be apart for so long in any case: two years, three years, more? Would they really like to see each other again soon? Showing her Paris, in 1960, discovering the USSR with her, in 1963, these had been great celebrations. This time he had not experienced the same jubilation, except at the beginning. He loved her very much, and she reciprocated, but they saw the world in such different ways; and neither of them really had a place in the other's life. The charming romantic impressions that he had when he first arrived had fizzled out little by little. It was stupid to have upset Nicole without a good reason, all for the sake of a casual exchange of words: 'You have nothing special to do in Paris, do you? – Nothing.'

'When it comes down to it, it was silly to extend our stay,' he said.

'It's silly if it doesn't even give you pleasure,' she said.

'So you regret it then?'

'I regret it if you do.'

Fine. They were going to go around in circles again. Something had become jammed in their dialogue; they each took wrongly, to some degree, what the other said. Would they never manage to break out of that? Why should they manage it today rather than yesterday? There was no reason.

They passed under a portico and in front of a church, which Nicole photographed. A little further on, another church with complicated architecture rose from the top of a hill. It dominated the Moskva, beyond which one could see a vast plain, and Moscow, in the distance. They sat down in the grass and looked at the view.

'That's it. On the one occasion when we are alone, we find nothing to say to each other. We don't even want to talk to each other,' Nicole thought bitterly. She had thought it would amuse André if they took some photos of Moscow together; the postcards were so bad. And he had lost interest in it; it had even seemed to annoy him. She stretched out on the grass, closed her eyes and suddenly she was ten years old: she was lying down in a meadow, with that smell of soil and greenery against her cheek. Why was a childhood memory so moving? Because time stretched out infinitely, the evening was becoming lost in the distance, and had eternity as its future. 'I know what I've missed in this country,' she told herself. Except for one night in Vladimir, nothing had touched her profoundly because nothing awoke resonances in her. The moments in her life that had moved her were always those which evoked something other than themselves; they seemed to her like a reminiscence, a premonition, the materialisation of a dream, a painting that had come to life, the image of a reality that, in itself, was inaccessible and mysterious. In the USSR, not only did she have no roots, but she had not loved it at a distance as she had Italy or Greece. That was why, here, even beautiful things were never anything more than what they were. She could admire them: she was not enchanted by them. Would André understand that? she wondered. She told herself morosely that it would not interest him.

But, all the same, for them to be alone together as she had so much wanted and yet not even profit from it was too depressing.

'I have just understood why nothing in the USSR moves me very much,' she said.

'Why?' he said.

He was so much present, so attentive – with everyone, but even more so with her – that she was astonished that she had hesitated to talk to him. It was easy, in the warmth of his look, to explain out loud what she had said to herself privately.

'In short, this trip has disappointed us both a little,' he said.

'Not you.'

'Yes, in a different way. Too many things have eluded me. I'm no further on than when we arrived. I shall be glad to be back in Paris.' He looked at her a little reproachfully: 'Although I haven't been bored: I'm never bored when I'm with you.'

'And I'm not when I'm with you, either.'

'Come on! You shouted it out at me: "I'm bored!"'

There was real sadness in his voice. She had shouted out her words in anger; she had forgotten them. And he seemed to have been deeply wounded by them. She hesitated, then decided.

'The truth is that I'm very fond of Macha, but seeing you when you're with her isn't at all the same as seeing you on your own. What bored me was never being alone with you. That made no difference to you, but it did to me,' she added a little bitterly.

'But there were many moments when we were alone.'

'Not many. And you threw yourself into your Russian grammar book.'

'You only had to talk to me.'

'You didn't want me to.'

'Funny! I had the impression that we were seeing more of each other than in Paris.'

'But always with Macha.'

'You seemed to be getting along so well with her: I didn't think that she was getting you down.'

'I get along with her. But when there is a third person between us, it's not the same thing.'

He gave a strange smile: 'That's what I often tell myself when you bring Philippe on our weekends away.'

She was disconcerted. Yes, she often asked Philippe to go with them; it seemed quite natural.

'That's quite different.'

'Because he's my son? He's still a third person between us.'

'He won't be any more.'

'That obviously upsets you a great deal!'

Were they going to argue again?

'No mother likes her son getting married. But you needn't think that it will make me ill.'

They were silent. No. We must not fall back into silence.

'Why did you never tell me that you sometimes found Philippe's presence a nuisance?'

'You've so often reproached me for being exclusive!

And then what would I have gained by depriving you of Philippe if I'm not enough for you in any case?'

'What do you mean, you're not enough for me?'

'Oh, you're happy to have me in your life. Provided that you have other things: your son, friends, Paris . . .'

'What you're saying is stupid,' she said, astonished. 'You need other things than me, too.'

'I can do without everything if I have you. I'd be perfectly happy alone with you, living in the country. You told me one day that you would die of boredom there.'

Was his dream of retiring to Villeneuve more serious than she thought?

'You prefer the country and I prefer Paris, because we all love the place where we spent our childhood.'

'That's not the real reason. I'm not enough for you and when I told you that the other day, you didn't even protest.'

She remembered. She was angry. And she had always had difficulty when she was knotted up and stiff with anger – in getting out the words that he needed.

'I was angry. I wasn't going to declare my love for you. But if you don't think that I am as attached to you as you are to me, then you're really stupid.'

She smiled tenderly. And there was some truth in what she was saying: Macha had scarcely left their side.

'In short,' he said, 'there has been a misunderstanding.'

'Yes. You thought I was bored with you, whereas I was bored of being without you: that's more flattering.'

'And I was happy to have you all to myself, but you didn't realise it.'

'But why did we misunderstand each other so badly?' she asked.

'Our disappointment put us in a bad mood. All the more so since we didn't want to admit it to ourselves.'

'We should always admit everything, to ourselves and to each other,' said Nicole.

'Do you always admit everything to me?'

She hesitated: 'Almost. And you?'

'Almost.'

They laughed together. Why had they been incapable of living together during the past few days? Everything seemed so familiar and so easy once again.

'There is one thing that I haven't told you, and which mattered,' she went on. 'Since I arrived in Moscow, I've grown old. I've realised that I have so little time left to live: that makes the slightest setbacks intolerable. You don't feel your age, but I do.'

'Oh, I feel it,' he said. 'I even think about it very often.'

'Is that true? You never talk about it.'

'That's in order not to make you sad. You don't talk about it, either.'

For a while, they remained silent. But it was no longer the same silence: just a pause in their finally-renewed dialogue, which would not stop any more. 'Shall we go back?' she asked.

'Let's go back.'

He took her arm. It's a great stroke of luck, to be able to talk to each other, she told herself. It's understandable that, with couples who don't know how to use words, misunderstandings should build up and end up spoiling everything between them.

'I was rather afraid that something had been spoiled between us.'

'Me, too.'

'But, basically, that was impossible,' he said.

'It was inevitable that we should end up by explaining things to each other.'

'Yes, it was inevitable. Next time, I won't be afraid again.'

He gripped her arm: 'There won't be a next time.'

Perhaps there would be one. But that was not important:

they would never again go very far astray from each other. He had not told her absolutely everything that had passed through his mind during the days concerned. And she had perhaps kept little things to herself. That was not important, either. They had found each other again. He would ask questions and she would reply.

'Why did you start feeling old?' he asked.

VINTAGE CLASSICS

Vintage launched in the United Kingdom in 1990, and was originally the paperback home for the Random House Group's literary authors. Now, Vintage comprises some of London's oldest and most prestigious literary houses, including Chatto & Windus (1855), Hogarth (1917), Jonathan Cape (1921) and Secker & Warburg (1935), alongside the newer or relaunched hardback and paperback imprints: The Bodley Head, Harvill Secker, Yellow Jersey, Square Peg, Vintage Paperbacks and Vintage Classics.

From Angela Carter, Graham Greene and Aldous Huxley to Toni Morrison, Haruki Murakami and Virginia Woolf, Vintage Classics is renowned for publishing some of the greatest writers and thinkers from around the world and across the ages – all complemented by our beautiful, stylish approach to design. Vintage Classics' authors have won many of the world's most revered literary prizes, including the Nobel, the Booker, the Prix Goncourt and the Pulitzer, and through their writing they continue to capture imaginations, inspire new perspectives and incite curiosity.

In 2007 Vintage Classics introduced its distinctive red spine design, and in 2012 Vintage Children's Classics was launched to include the much-loved authors of our childhood. Random House joined forces with the Penguin Group in 2013 to become Penguin Random House, making it the largest trade publisher in the United Kingdom.

@vintagebooks

penguin.co.uk/vintage-classics